The Winter Foursome

By

Chad Wannamaker

COPYRIGHT@2021

THE WINTER FOURSOME

DISCLAIMER

This story is for adults only. It is written to arouse and entertain. **Do not read this story if you are offended by explicit descriptions of adults engaging in various forms of consensual sex.**

This is a work of fiction. Names, characters, places, and incidents are either the product of the author's imagination or are used fictitiously, and any resemblance to actual persons, living or dead, business establishments, events, or location is entirely coincidental.

THE WINTER FOURSOME

Copyright

In no way is it legal to reproduce, duplicate, or transmit any part of this document in either electronic means or in printed format. Recording of this publication is strictly prohibited and any storage of this document is not allowed unless with written permission from the publisher. All rights reserved.

The information provided herein is stated to be truthful and consistent, in that any liability, in terms of inattention or otherwise, by any usage or abuse of any policies, processes, or directions contained within is the solitary and utter responsibility of the recipient reader. Under no circumstances will any legal responsibility or blame be held against the publisher for any reparation, damages, or monetary loss due to the information herein, either directly or indirectly.

Respective authors own all copyrights not held by the publisher. The information herein is offered for informational purposes solely, and is universal as so. The presentation of the information is without contract or any type of guarantee assurance.

The trademarks that are used are without any consent, and the publication of the trademark is without permission or backing by the trademark owner. All trademarks and brands within this book are for clarifying purposes only and are the owned by the owners themselves, not affiliated with this document.

THE WINTER FOURSOME

CHAPTER I:
THE OPENING

"Oh fuck, oh shit... YES!"

Donald grunted loudly before pulling his dick out. He was cumming already. Terry watched him as he stroked himself quickly. Several shots of semen flew out of his cock landing on her tight stomach. It was a good-sized load, she thought, maybe a little more than normal.

"Ohhhhh, yeah... fuck yes," Donald said as she pushed out the last drop. "I'm sorry."

Terry looked up at him and smiled. She lovingly rubbed his thigh. "It's okay babe. We aren't just having a fling with each other," she said.

"I thought I could go a lot longer than that. Then it just kinda happened," Donald said, still holding his softening cock.

"I'm serious, it's fine. Don't worry about it. We need to pack anyway."

Donald lay down next to Terry as they both looked up at the ceiling. They had been married for four years and dated for five before that. While they were still madly in

THE WINTER FOURSOME

love with one another, their life together was entering a new phase. They wanted to have children. At least two. The days of clubbing, late night parties, and spontaneous traveling were quickly coming to an end. Realizing this, they both wanted to enjoy as much of this life as they could before it was time to really settle down.

"How long do you think it'll take to get up there?" Terry asked, as she used her fingers to play with Donald's cum.

"Depends on traffic. Three, maybe four, hours I'd say." Donald replied.

The couple was headed to Maine with their friends Kristal and Peter. They all planned on spending a few days at a ski cabin they rented online.

"Can you believe one of these is going to be our little baby?" Terry said as she held up a glob of cum in her hand.

Donald looked at it and smiled. "Clearly not that one, huh?" he joked.

"Are you just gonna lie there or actually get me a towel?" Terry said as she shoved Donald playfully when he got up.

THE WINTER FOURSOME

"C'mon, let's shower. We still need to pack and get out of here," Donald said, wiping his cum off her stomach.

He took a minute to throw some of his things in a suitcase, giving Terry a head start in the shower. As he opened the bathroom door, he stopped to admire his wife through the glass shower door. She was truly stunning. At roughly 168 cm, she had an athletic and toned frame as a result of playing many sports growing up. Her breasts were larger than average and still very much hearty and youthful.

Terry reached around her back and washed her round firm ass with a pink loofah. Soap suds streamed down her crack, legs, and onto her cute feet. Her caramel skin shined from the suds. She leaned her head back and closed her eyes as she soaked her long and voluminous dark hair.

My wife is so fucking hot, Donald thought to himself.

While Terry maintained a very fit body, Donald was not so driven. His 33 years on Earth had started to catch up to him. He was slightly taller than Terry at 173 cm with brown hair and dark eyes. He also sported a neatly trimmed beard.

THE WINTER FOURSOME

Donald was handsome, outgoing, funny, and full of charm. That is what drew Terry to him in the first place. But years of traveling for work, minimal exercise, and poor eating resulted in some extra weight. While most wouldn't look at him and say he was fat, almost no one would say he was in shape. Quite literally everyone, however, would agree Terry is in another league compared to Donald.

Donald and Terry both had well paying full-time jobs. It allowed them to afford a beautiful home with fabulous amenities. Donald stepped into their double shower, which was plenty large enough for the both of them. Terry turned to face Donald, her hands rubbing shampoo through her hair.

"Do I need to shave?" She asked.

"There's a hot tub there, I'm pretty sure," said Donald, looking down at her legs.

Terry made a sad face. "I really don't feel like shaving."

Donald shrugged. "Okay, but don't complain when everyone calls you a werewolf."

THE WINTER FOURSOME

She splashed him playfully, before reaching past him to grab her razor.

"Kristal and Peter are bringing all the booze and have a bunch of breakfast stuff too, right? So I guess we'll do lunches and dinners?" Donald asked as he soaped up his chest and arms.

"That's fine, that's easy," she said, moving from her legs to her bikini area. She meticulously shaved her pubic hair as not to remove it all, but to instead trim it neatly.

Donald watched closely as his wife groomed her pubes. "I like when you leave some hair there."

"A shaved vag is so 2007," she joked.

The combination of washing his penis and watching Terry shave had led Donald to achieve another erection rather quickly.

"Hey," he said, holding his penis in one hand.

"What?" Terry asked, looking up at Donald, before quickly realizing he was hard. "Oh, my God, really? You literally just came."

THE WINTER FOURSOME

Donald smiled and shrugged. "I like watching you shave, what can I say?"

Terry reached out and grabbed his penis by the tip. Donald had a realtivly small penis. It was probably no more than four inches long, and maybe three inches in girth. Terry always thought it got smaller as the years went on, but that was most likely due to Donald gaining some weight. She didn't care, however. She loved everything about him.

"You like my small dick?"

"It's not small at all."

Donald laughed. "It absolutely is."

"Well, I like it. And I wouldn't trade it for the world," she said, holding it in her hand.

Terry dropped his penis and finished rinsing her hair.

"Hey, what gives? Can you help me out?" he asked, seeing that she was continuing with her routine.

"You're being serious? You need to cum again?" She asked with a surprised look on her face.

THE WINTER FOURSOME

Donald smiled and nodded. "What can I say, my wife is hot."

"Thank you, honey. But we need to go. Not enough time for round two," she said as she exited the shower.

"Ugh, fine. But I'm gonna jerk off in here!" Donald called out.

"Suit yourself!" She yelled back to him from the bedroom.

Terry truly didn't mind. That's what being together nine years had done.

Donald was disappointed that he got blue balls, but he had no real intentions of masturbating. He quickly wrapped up his shower, dried off, and finished packing.

CHAPTER II:
THE RIDE

The ride to the mountains was uneventful. There was little to no traffic and driving conditions were good. Donald enjoyed the quiet time as Terry, per usual, slept almost the whole way. He looked over at her repeatedly as she curled up on her side in the passenger seat. She was wearing black leggings, tan Ugg boots, and a North Face fleece. Her hair draped neatly down the sides of her face, spilling out of her winter hat. *She looked adorable*, Donald thought to himself.

As they neared their destination, Terry slowly opened her eyes. She looked around trying to recognize something. "Whoa, are we almost there?" she asked as she straightened up in her seat.

"Yep. You slept pretty much the whole way. It says we'll be there in fifteen minutes."

"Amazing," Terry said as she stretched her arms up as high as she could. "I'm sorry I wasn't much company."

"It's okay. But you did miss out on the World War II podcast. It was a good one."

THE WINTER FOURSOME

Terry rolled her eyes. "Oh, bummer. Really wish I caught that one," she said, picking a piece of lint off his sweatshirt.

As they pulled into the driveway of their mountainside rental, Peter and Kristal were already unloading their car. Kristal gave an enthusiastic wave as they pulled up.

"Great timing!" shouted Donald as he rolled down his window, pulling up next to Peter's car.

"Hey guys!" shouted Kristal as she ran over to Terry's side of the car. Kristal and Terry had been close friends since starting a job together after college. They worked side by side for four years before Kristal left for another company. But they have remained close.

Kristal had tan skin and jet black hair. Her eyes were big and green. Sporting a thin frame and very large natural breasts, Kristal could always turn a few heads. She hugged Terry almost before she could get out of the car.

"I'm so excited!" she said. "Hey Donald!"

"Hey, Kristal!" Donald said, with his attention on unloading the car. Peter was busy unloading their skis from the roof carrier.

THE WINTER FOURSOME

"Hey Peter," Donald said as he approached him, carrying two suitcases.

"How you doing, Donald?"

"I'm doing good. We're happy to get out here for a vacation."

Donald and Peter were cordial with one another but wouldn't be considered friends per se. While Donald was normally the outgoing and boisterous type, Peter was much more reserved, stoic in his mannerisms and behavior. In contrast to Donald, he was tall at 188cm with a muscular frame, broad shoulders, and big hands. He always carried himself with certainty and confidence.

"You guys, wait until you see how much alcohol we picked up!" Kirstal said with a big smile on her face. She rushed around Peter's car and opened the trunk. Inside were six cases of beer, two boxes filled with wine bottles, vodka, tequila, and bourbon. "You think this is enough for four people?"

"That's enough for forty!" said Terry, as Kristal took a sip of beer, she already had in her hand. "Please tell me you weren't drinking that on the way up." Terry said with an annoyed look on her face.

Kristal shrugged as she took another sip. "I wasn't driving," she said as she winked at her friend. "C'mon, let's go check out the place."

"You know it doesn't matter that you weren't driving right?" Terry replied.

"Ya, I know. Buuuut... I didn't get caught, so it doesn't count." Kristal replied with a smile. "Now MOM, can we please go and check this place out."

Terry just chuckled with her friend and said, "sure."

The house was large. It was situated on the side of a mountain, and the rental included the fees for the ski lift tickets. That would allow the four of them to ski whenever they'd like, without having to drive to the lodge. The living room had a very tall ceiling with a huge fireplace. The open concept gave way to a modern elaborate kitchen, complete with a pizza brick oven and espresso maker. There was a large deck off the living room. The deck sported a jacuzzi and seating area with large heat lamps.

THE WINTER FOURSOME

"This place is incredible!" shouted Kristal, rushing from room to room. "Look, a jacuzzi!"

Peter had walked to the basement after placing the contents from his car inside. He emerged from the basement. "Hey guys, there's a sauna down there."

"Like, a sauna sauna?" asked Kristal.

Peter nodded. "Crazy right? This place is great."

Terry and Donald took their bags upstairs into one of the bedrooms. As they entered the room Donald tossed his bag into the closed, kicked off his shoes, and sprawled out on the bed. Terry, on the other hand, chose to neatly unpack her things organizing them in the dresser, and hanging clothes in the closet. She looked at Donald and smiled. He obviously had no interest in unpacking.

"I like you in your little ski bunny outfit you've got going on here," he said as she bent over to collect her things. "You've got this nice little 'innocent suburban girl in the mountains' look to you."

Terry rolled her eyes. "I like this fleece. It's so comfortable."

THE WINTER FOURSOME

"Come here for a second," he said, putting his hand to his crotch again.

Terry grabbed her phone and plopped down on the bed next to him. She looked down at his apparent erection, then back at him. "Again? I thought you jerked off in the shower!"

"No, no, I never did. Was saving it for us. We should christen this place you know."

Terry giggled and lowered her voice. "We literally just got here. And they're walking around right now," she nodded towards the door. "We're not having sex."

"C'mon, Terry. Please? I am really horny right now. You're killing me in these little black leggings!" said Donald with a playful growl.

Terry, still playing on her phone, rolled her eyes. She sat her phone down on her chest and looked at Donald. "Fine, I'll jerk you off."

"Yes!" said Donald as he quickly unbuckled his pants and pulled them down. Terry helped him pull his underwear down, freeing his hard dick. She said, "you better not take forever," as she slowly moved her head down to his erect cock. She slowly licked around the head of his penis, making sure to soak it with saliva. She took his entire length into her mouth, holding it there for a few seconds. Donald gave out a low groan of pleasure. As she took his warm throbbing cock out of her mouth, she spat a large glob of saliva into her hand and started stroking his shaft.

Terry's hands were small and slender, but Donald's dick didn't leave much runway to stroke. She began her handjob sliding up and down, past the head each time. Donald leaned back and exhaled deeply. He spread his legs as Terry worked her magic.

Terry's hand was doing most of the work while she rested her head on Donald's thigh. They both looked down at her stroking his cock, all the while listening to Peter and Kristal talking downstairs. Terry was excited to join them, and it was clear she was bored and unamused by her current activity. She was hoping that Donald was going to have a speedy orgasm.

"Feel good?" she whispered, sensing his breathing increase.

And then, on cue, Donald muffled a groan as she continued to stroke his throbbing penis, and shot out a glob of cum onto his belly. Terry lifted her head up and leaned out of the way as the second salvo landed on Donald's chest.

"Fuck," he whispered as he shot more onto his chest. Terry kept stroking as two more smaller bursts dribbled out of his cock's head. Donald laughed as his orgasm subsided.

Terry smiled and got up from the bed, careful to not touch anything with her saliva and cum-covered hand. She went to the bathroom to clean up while Donald leaned back and closed his eyes.

Terry came back with a towel and tossed it to Donald. His cock had already retracted to its two-inch flaccid state. Terry watched him clean up his cum.

"I'm surprised you had that much left after this morning," she said with a smirk on her face. "You're a little hornball today, huh?"

Donald grinned as he finished cleaning up. "I told you. My wife is fuckin' hot! That's what it is."

Terry smiled, leaned over and kissed her husband. "Okay, pull your pants up hornball. I'll see you downstairs."

THE WINTER FOURSOME

"Okay, give me a few minutes and I'll be down."

CHAPTER III:
DINNER TIME

The two couples hung out, relaxing and catching up in front of the fireplace. The fire had a low glowing roar, and the White Ash wood was filling the cabin with a wonderful soft fragrance. It was relaxing to be out of the car and in the comfortable environment of the cabin amongst friends. Donald was especially enjoying himself, as he stole several peeks at Kristal. He found her to be a different kind of hot, compared to Terry. With her smooth silky skin, piercing green eyes, and flowing black hair, it was easy to see the attraction. She sat in an armchair sideways with her legs hanging off the side, giggling with the flow of conversation. Donald thought it was adorable.

"It's almost six. I'm gonna go get ready for dinner," Kristal announced to the group, breaking through the laughter of funny stories.

"But… dinner's at seven-thirty though," said Donald with a confused look.

"Boys will never understand what it takes to maintain this level of beauty," said Kristal, as she jokingly pretended to pose for a picture.

Donald took this opportunity to get a good look at Kristal's whole body. Standing there in all her glory.
"Well, I'm gonna to headup and get ready too," Terry said as she stood up, noticing that Donald wasn't staring her.

Terry followed Kristal upstairs to get ready while Donald and Peter sat by the fire, drinking beers.

"How's work, man?" Donald asked, hoping to create some conversation.

"It's good. I've been keeping busy, ya know. How about you?"

"Uhh... pretty much the same thing," Donald replied while looking down into his beer bottle, before taking another sip. Creating conversation with Peter was proving difficult.

"Bucs are looking good this year, huh?" said Peter taking another sip from his beer. Football was the only common ground the two had.

"They sure are. That team is stacked, and Brady's playing like he's twenty-five too. It's kinda crazy that he's still going at forty-three," said Donald, as he sipped his beer.

THE WINTER FOURSOME

The two continued chatting about the state of the NFL season.

*****

"I like those jeans," Terry said as Kristal leaned over the sink applying makeup. Terry brought in a few outfits from her room to choose from for herself, and she laid them out on Kristal's bed.

"Thanks! They're new. Christmas gift from Peter." Kristal said applying her makeup wearing a pair of jeans and a lace black bra. Her large breasts hung perfectly from her slim frame over the sink. She stood on her tippy toes to get close to the mirror.

Terry debated over the outfit selections she had laid out as Kristal walked over and stood next to her. "The first one," Kristal said with conviction. "That's cute."

"You think?" Terry asked as she held it up to herself, looking in the mirror. "It is, isn't it."

"For sure," said Kristal as she put on a green and black flannel shirt.

THE WINTER FOURSOME

As Terry tried on her shirt, she eyed an open suitcase on the floor, next to the mirror. It appeared to be Peter's suitcase. In it, he had neatly folded shirts, pants, underwear, and socks. His Dopp kit was packed into the suitcase but open. That's when Terry noticed something.

Inside his Dopp kit, clearly visible, was a small box of condoms. But not just any condoms. The brand read 'Trojan Magnum XL.' Terry and Donald hadn't used condoms in years, especially lately as they wanted to get pregnant. But when they did, Donald never used Magnum XL or even Magnum for that matter.

She looked over at Kristal who was busy picking out shoes. The she looked back down at the suitcase to confirm what she saw.

XL? she thought to herself. *How big is he?*

Terry felt flush and slightly guilty for snooping in his bag, but it was already open, so it was free game. She quickly put her outfit on and told Kristal she'd see her downstairs.

*****

THE WINTER FOURSOME

The foursome went out to dinner at a nice Italian restaurant in the ski village. They had a nice meal and told more funny stories. Afterwards, they hit a small local bar, played some pool, and had some beers before heading back to the cabin.

As they walked into the cabin, Donald grabbed a bottle of whiskey, cracked it open, and poured shots for everyone. Peter turned up the radio, and today's hits started blasting through the Bluetooth subwoofer. Their first night in Maine was shaping up to be quite a success.

"Time for some shits!" Donald shouted to the group. "I meant shots," he said laughingly correcting himself.

"I don't know if you need anymore alcohol babe," Terry said with a huge smile.

"I'm fine, I'm fine. It was just a slip of the tongue."

"Well let's see what else that tongue can slip on later babe," Terry replied with smirk.

They all gathered around the fire and started taking their shots.

*****

THE WINTER FOURSOME

"You are absolutely lying. We probably have sex once a week, at best!" said Donald as he threw another log on the fire.

Terry laughed. "Okay, okay, you're probably right. But lately, we've upped our game, wouldn't you say?"

"I'm not so sure about that one." said Donald with a skeptical look.

"Umm... we literally just had sex this morning!" Terry argued.

Kristal said through her emphatic laughter, "she's got you there, Donald."

"Well, I mean, c'mon. We're trying to make a human, Kristal." The group laughed.

"Well, I can honestly say we are probably an every nighter," Kristal said looking at Peter. "Right, babe? I feel like we definitely put up some good numbers. Well, unless I need some recovery time!" joked Kristal.

"Yeah, we do alright," said Peter, smiling as he took a sip of his freshly made Old Fashioned.

THE WINTER FOURSOME

"Recovery time?" asked Terry, with confusion.

"Well, yeah! I need to rest the va-jay-jay sometimes!"

Terry nodded, pretending to agree. But the truth was, she didn't find sex to be particularly painful at all. "Very true," she said plainly. "Babe, I guess we'll have to work on our numbers then, huh?"

"I'm ready when you are!"

"Okay!" said Kristal, breaking the direction of the conversation by loudly slapping her legs and standing up. "I'm putting my bathing suit on. It's Jacuzzi time."

"Ooo, ooo me too!" Terry jumped up and followed her. "This is going to be so much fun!"

CHAPTER IV:
HEATING UP

Both women looked absolutely stunning in their bikinis. Terry wore a bright yellow tow-piece MIKOH bikini, showcasing her perfect curves and toned stomach. The bikini had cheeky bottoms that accentuated her round buttocks. She dipped her toe in the water to test the temperature before descending into the water. Kristal followed her, opting for a bright red two-piece Victoria's Secret bikini. Her large boobs formed breathtaking cleavage in her V-cut bikini top. Her thong bottoms completed the immaculate picture. It was impossible for Donald not to notice how hot she looked. He tried his hardest not to stare, but successfully snuck in many long, hard looks at her breasts. He tried to get peeks at her bottom in those thongs, but she entered the water facing him.

Meanwhile, Peter sported white swim trunks that looked to be perhaps a size too small for him. He didn't seem to mind as he approached the Jacuzzi with confidence, handing out drinks to everyone who was already inside.

"The water's so nice, but the air is so cold," Kristal giggled as she crossed her arms, covering her breasts as best she could.

THE WINTER FOURSOME

"I know, it's gotta be like thirty degrees out," Terry said as she looked up at Peter. "Are those heat lamps? Peter, you think you can grab one while you're up there?"

"No problem," he said as he walked over to the heat lamp and pulled it over closer to the Jacuzzi. As he worked on setting it up, he had to reach up to where the power switch was. Everyone watched as he figured out how to activate the lamp. Terry's eyes wandered to Peter's crotch area while he was focused on the lamp. Peter's trunks were white and clung tightly to his body. There was nothing left to the imagination. Terry eyed what appeared to be a long and thick penis, situated snugly against his thigh. It was enormous. Even in the dim light of the deck, she could clearly make out the head of his cock which appeared bulbous and profound.

Donald easily noticed it too. He couldn't believe this guy was packing that much. He was certain Peter was still soft, yet had a penis considerably larger than Donald's was even when hard. Donald looked at Terry and could clearly see her eyes were glued to Peter's crotch. She was loving this. Donald looked back at Peter still fiddling with the switch. He pictured Kristal having sex with Peter's giant dick for a few seconds. *Get out of my head*, Donald thought to himself.

THE WINTER FOURSOME

"Ok, got it!" said Peter as he stepped back and looked at the glowing heat lamp. "That was a lot more confusing than I thought it'd be."

"Okay, get in here now. Hurry, it's freezing!" Kristal shouted as Peter descended the steps right next to Terry. His cock was even more on display as he maneuvered down the steps. Donald noticed Terry was incredibly intentional about not looking at it.

The conversation flowed again as the group was relaxing in the Jacuzzi. It was obvious Terry was particularly interested in Peter as she carried on talking to him, seemingly very interested in what he had to say. Donald picked up on this, but didn't see it in any way alarming because everyone was having a great time including him. At one point, Kristal and Peter got close to each other and were talking very quietly. Kristal was giggling as Peter whispered in her ear. Things seemed to be heating up.

"Hey guys, we're gonna turn in," Kristal said, lightly shoving Peter aside to give herself some space. "It's been a long day and night."

"Yeah, we're probably right behind you guys. Starting to get kinda drunk. We'll see you tomorrow."

THE WINTER FOURSOME

Kristal and Peter ascended the steps. This time, Terry didn't hide her gaze as she stared directly at Peter's imprint. It looked even bigger than before, likely because he was growing an erection from whatever he and Kristal were talking about earlier. Donald and Terry hung back in the Jacuzzi, talking and finishing their drinks before they too decided to head upstairs.

Donald laid in bed reading his phone while Terry brushed her teeth. The electric brush made some noise, but it Donald could still hear the other couple talking and giggling quietly through the wall. The walls were so thin that he could almost make out what they were saying. Terry hopped into bed and snuggled up with Donald. As they laid in silence, the room became filled with the sounds of Peter and Kristal next door.

"They're having fun, huh?" Terry asked as she snuggled up tighter with Donald.

"They sure are. I wonder how long they'll be up?" Donald replied while staring at the celing.

Then, after some silence, it started. Kristal and Peter's bed started rocking, slowly at first. Terry looked up at Donald, smiling. They knew what was happening in the next room. The rocking increased in pace and intensity. That's when they started to hear her.

"Oh, ohhh, ohhhhh," Kristal moaned, loud enough for everyone to hear. "Oh God, Peter... oh fuck, Peter... yes... ohhhh..."

Terry signed 'shh' by placing her index finger over her mouth as she fought back her giggles.

"Oh, my... ohhh fuck, it's so big... Oh yes baby, this pussy is all yours. Tear it up, Peter."

Terry knew Donald clearly heard Kristal say how big it was, but she didn't look at him or even acknowledge what she heard. She continued to snuggle with him as they listened to their weekend roommates having sex.

Terry slowly started to kiss on Donald's neck and ran the edges of her nails across his chest. He didn't follow along with her plans though. Donald just laid there, and gently rubbed on Terry's arm. She stopped trying to initiate an equally passionate vibe to combat the great sex they heard coming from the next room.

The sex next door, and lack of sex in their room, went on seemingly for forever. Eventually, Terry and Donald grew tired enough and they tried to get to sleep. But it was impossible to sleep with the constant banging and moaning from their friend's room.

"Fuck, fuck, oh, fuck, yes, oh, hell yes, don't stop baby, YES, YES, OHHHH PETER!!"

Clearly orgasming next door, Kristal's voice filled their room with her shouts. She was either too drunk to be a little quieter, or simply didn't care that anyone else could heard her. Then the sound of a deep and powerful grunt came as Peter apparently reached an orgasm also.

"Argggghhhhhhh!" he shouted as Kristal continued to moan over him. The two of them orgasmed together for a good fifteen seconds, before there was finally silence except for a very light giggling and talking.

Terry didn't say anything as she laid with her eyes closed. Donald could tell from her breathing that she wasn't asleep yet, and he knew she heard what he had heard. He had wondered if she heard the part about Peter being big. He wondered what she thought of that.

The live action from next door ignited something within Donald. The sex session he heard gave him a throbbing erection. But even though he was rock hard, he tried to

THE WINTER FOURSOME

fight off the mental imagery of Kristal getting pounded by Peter's huge dick. He wanted the erection to go away. He was too apprehensive to try and pleasure Terry after hearing that. In time it worked, and Donald drifted off to sleep.

Terry lying there with her eyes closed but still awake, pictured what it must have been like for Kristal to have sex with Peter. She was screaming almost the whole time. She lost count of how many times she guessed she orgasmed. She kept picturing what Peter's cock looked like, plunging in and out of Kristal's pussy. Images of him in those soaking wet white trunks, fixing the light, repeatedly flashed in her mind. She knew she was getting so wet, but didn't dare touch herself. Eventually, she calmed down enough to drift off to sleep in her husband's arms.

*****

Donald reclined in his beach chair as Kristal and Terry sat on either side of him. They were both wearing matching black one-piece bikinis, but Donald was naked and sporting a throbbing erection. Kristal held his penis as she sipped her drink and chatted with Terry. Every once in a while she would stroke it up and down, but then go back to just holding it. Dozens of beachgoers walked by, but they didn't seem to notice anything happening or simply didn't care.

Donald desperately wanted her to keep stroking, but she wouldn't. She was too preoccupied with her conversation to take notice, and Terry just ignored the whole situation. He needed to cum but couldn't unless she kept going. No matter what Donald tried, she wouldn't move her hand. It was no use, she was purposely denying his orgasim. *It must be some type of new game she's trying, but I really want to cum*, Donald thought to himself. She slowly started to stroke it more and more as Terry was taking a drink of her cocktail, then suddenly... Donald's eyes snapped open to find Terry curled up next to him. *It was a damn dream*, and Terry was wide awake, waiting for Donald to open his eyes.

"Good morning," she said softly.

"Hey, how long have you been up?" he said sleepily.

"Not long. Just waiting for you to get up... well, the rest of you that is."

Donald looked down and saw that he had a raging hard-on, and Terry's hand was wrapped around it, stroking up

THE WINTER FOURSOME

and down softly. "You were sound asleep with this thing." She said with a smile.

Donald closed his eyes as he let Terry slowly stroke his cock. She teased him a little by kissing his stomach, thighs, and then lightly licking his balls. She came back up to his face after a minute or two. While looking longingly into his eyes, she whispered, "I wanna fuck baby."

"Gladly," Donald replied as he leaned over to kiss her. She stopped him before he got to her lips with her index finger.

"Uh-uh-uh, go brush," she said sternly.

Donald frowned. "Really?"

Terry nodded and moved back to her side of the bed to show she was serious. Begrudgingly, he got out of bed and wandered off to the bathroom wearing nothing but a t-shirt. Terry giggled a little as his boner bounced left and right while he was walking. She sprawled out in the bed and slipped her hand in her panties. She slowly massaged her clit and closed her eyes, picturing Peter's bulge. She was so incredibly horny, she felt like she could orgasm in seconds.

THE WINTER FOURSOME

Donald came hurrying back and jumped in bed on top of Terry. She let out a playful shriek as he devoured her face. As they made out, Donald grabbed healthy handfuls of her boobs. He smelled her hair, that had a light fragrance of lilac, while slowly rubbing her nipples as he kissed the sides of her face. He rubbed his hard cock against her stomach. Terry grabbed a hold of it and responded by stroking it. She spread her legs and looked into Donald's eyes, "I wanna cum so bad," she whispered.

"Oh, you do. I want you to cum all over my dick. I love to feel you pulsate around it."

Donald grabbed his dick and slowly pressed it into her soaked pussy. Terry opened her mouth and closed her eyes as she took him in. Thrust after thrust, her breathing intensified. After roughly two minutes, she began to orgasm. As she reached her creamy climax, she put her hand over her mouth to muffle her moans. Donald couldn't believe how quickly she came. She normally only reached a speedy climax from oral or with toys. As he watched her orgasm take over her body in a way he had never seen before, he felt his own orgasm rush through his body.

THE WINTER FOURSOME

"Oh fuck, I'm gonna cum," he announced. "Where do you want it?"

Terry still had her hand over her mouth. She removed it and stifled a whisper between moans, "Inside. I want you to fill me up baby." Instantly, he unloaded all of his of cum inside her. He grunted loudly to which Terry immediately covered his mouth while giggling. Donald thrusted hard as he ejaculated inside her. After one final push, he relaxed his body and rested on top of her. They kissed passionately as his penis began to soften inside of her.

"That was so good," she said lovingly. Donald smiled down at at her and got from on top of her. He leaned on one arm as he took a long gaze at her vagina. A thick glob of cum was leaking down to the sheets. He caught it with his finger and held it up. "These ones escaped," he said with a laugh as he pushed it inside of her with his finger.

Terry laughed and swatted him away, before leaning forward and looking for herself. "Am I supposed to, like, lean back and let them soak in or something?"

"Yeah, you're actually supposed to stand on your head or something for about five minutes. I read somewhere on the Internet that you're supposed to do that if you want it to work."

Terry rolled her eyes and smiled. "Oh ok, well then it must be true since it was on the internet."

Donald rested next to her. "Wow. Twice in two days. We really are working on upping our numbers, huh?"

"Mmm hmm. And don't forget about the handjob."

"That's right. Wow. You're a little hornball. Just like your husband!" he said as they laid there relaxing. They could hear the faint bustling of pots and pans downstairs.

"Ah, crap. They're making breakfast. Come on, let's go ahead and head down. Don't wanna be bad housemates!" Terry shouted as she jumped out of bed and headed for the bathroom.

CHAPTER V:
MORNING AFTER

Downstairs, Kristal and Peter buzzed about the kitchen getting breakfast ready. They had gotten up early and went for a snowy walk around the cabin. They were each still wearing their skin tight thermals from their walk.

"Look at you guys making breakfast. This is awesome!" Terry said as she approached and took a seat at the kitchen bar. Kristal walked over, smiling, and poured cups of coffee for Terry and Donald.

"Good morning you two," Kristal said with a small grin. Terry wondered if she had heard them having sex. "Peter and I got up and went walking all around this area. It's so beautiful. And it was a good workout too!"

Peter was busy working the stove, flipping bacon and scrambling eggs. "I guess they just got a bunch of snow the last couple of days," he said without turning around. "So skiing is gonna be great this weekend."

"I can't wait to get out there. You guys wanna go after breakfast?" Donald asked as walked to the bar and sat down. "This coffee is really good. I definitely needed this, long night."

THE WINTER FOURSOME

"Without a doubt," said Peter as he turned from the stove and placed some bacon on Terry and Donald's plates.

"Thanks, man, this is great," said Donald as he got ready to dig in.

"Look at you, Peter. I didn't know you could cook!" Terry said as she smiled up at him. Peter smiled back before turning to clean up the dishes. He was still wearing his thermal gear. While Kristal's outfit was black, Peter's was light gray. Terry couldn't help but notice his immense bulge visible under the snug layer of clothing. Even more pronounced than last night, Peter's thick cock held tightly against his leg, just begging for attention.

Terry was in somewhat of a trance. She definitely stared a split second too long before looking away. No one noticed her staring, but now she struggled to not look again. Donald was busy devouring the breakfast, and Kristal scrolled her phone. Terry figured it safe to take another good look. As Peter worked around the kitchen, she watched his huge penis whenever she could. She wondered to herself, *how big is it really. I wonder if it gets a lot bigger after it's hard.* Crammed in his pants, she could see it moving a little as Peter moved around the kitchen.

Okay, okay, that was enough. She had to stop. "Well, thank you Peter. Thanks Kristal. That was awesome. What a great treat to come down to," said Terry as she took her plate over to the dishwasher. "Looks like you guys are ready to go skiing, should we leave in fifteen?"

"Sounds good," said Donald as he quickly jumped up to help clean the kitchen and get ready. "I can't wait to hit the slopes."

*****

After a long day of skiing, the group decided to call it quits and hit the bar for some well-deserved drinks. They pulled into the North Peak Lodge, which happened to be pretty close to their cabin. They sat reminiscing about the day at a table near the bar.

"You're fast, Peter! I saw you coming down on the last run and didn't even realize it was you until you passed by me. You were like *zooooom!*" said Terry as the server dropped off a glass of red wine for her.

"Yeah I get in the zone, I guess. Sorry about that, I would have stopped."

"Oh no, don't be silly. I'm super slow anyway."

THE WINTER FOURSOME

"You guys cooked breakfast, so Terry and I will be making some bad ass lasagna tonight. Get ready, is all I'm saying," Donald said to the table.

"I can't wait. I'm starving and exhausted. Late night and big day today, huh?" said Kristal as she sipped her beer.

"Very late night," said Terry as she smiled at her.

Kristal buried her face in her hands and blushed. "Okay, okay, okay. Very funny. We were quiet and respectful."

"You were?" asked Donald, to which Peter almost spit out his beer he laughed so hard.

"Look, look, you guys, it's completely fine. We're all adults. We're here to have fun! Just remember, it's my credit card on file so, umm, go easy on that mattress will ya?" said Terry with big smile.

Kristal burst out laughing, still embarrassed as she held her head in her hands. Peter lovingly caressed her shoulders. "We will, we will. Don't you worry. Excuse me everyone, I need to hit the head," he said as he stood up to head to the bathroom. Terry immediately eyed his crotch again.

THE WINTER FOURSOME

"Me too," said Donald as he followed Peter to the bathroom.

As the two men stood side by side in the only two urinals, they continued their chat. "We were that loud, huh?" asked Peter.

Donald remained facing straight ahead as they continued their chat in the bathroom. "Yeah man, heh, you were. But ya know it's all good. I'm happy for you, bud."

After Peter was finished, he stepped back slightly and fiddled with his zipper. That's when Donald glanced down and accidentally saw it. Peter's penis hung lazily out of his underwear. It was enormous. Donald guessed it had to be at least seven inches or so. Peter grabbed it with his hand and stuffed it back into his pants. It appeared to be a nearly impossible task to get it back in.

"See ya out there," said Peter as he walked off.

Donald stood there, facing the wall. He was done urinating, but was too much in shock to move. What did he just see? He couldn't get it out of his mind. That was easily the biggest penis he's ever seen. He looked down at his soft penis. He held it using his thumb and index finger. He imagined Peter's soft penis was probably four times the size of his. Stunned, he put his dick back, washed his hands, and headed out to join the group.

"So would you guys want a boy or a girl?" asked Kristal as Donald sat back down.

"I think he wants a girl, but I want a boy, right babe? But honestly, it doesn't matter one bit. We just want a healthy baby."

Kristal nodded. "That's so cute, you guys. Very exciting news!"

"But hey, trying is one of the best parts," said Donald.

Kristal laughed. "Well, we all officially know the beds at this place can support the effort!" Everyone laughed.

"Oh, believe me, we made sure to test them ourselves," said Terry.

"Nice!" said Kristal. Peter and Donald high-fived.

"We didn't even hear you! Now that's stealth booty. Peter, we need to take a play out of their book, don't we."

"Don't look at me!" joked Peter. "You're the one screaming like you were in the opera."

"You could have muffled me or something!" she joked back.

"That's true, Peter. I did that for Donald," Terry said as she winked at him. Donald shifted uncomfortably in his seat.

"I'm not sure there's a volume control on you, babe. It's just stuck in a perpetually increasing mode." Said Peter, winking.

"Okay, you guys. Okay. You try and keep quiet when there's a ten-inch dick being jammed into you! Sheesh!" said Kristal.

Everyone laughed, but it was Kristal's last comment that stuck in the minds of Terry and Donald as the conversation moved on. Did she just declare Peter's penis to be ten inches? Seriously?! At first, Terry wasn't even sure she heard correctly. The conversation had moved well past the sex, so she didn't want to awkwardly bring it up again. She tried to picture in her head a ten-inch erect penis. She kept going back to the bulge in the pool and in the kitchen that morning.

THE WINTER FOURSOME

Donald couldn't stop thinking about it either. Here was this good looking guy, sharing confines with them for the whole weekend. And now his wife knew he had a ten-inch cock. He saw Peter's flaccid penis himself and knew it had to be true. He wasn't quite sure if he was jealous, embarrassed, or a little of both. But, either way, he desperately wondered what Terry thought about it.

"Ok, we ready to get out of here?" asked Kristal as the group finished their drinks. "I'm tired, anyone want to go back now?" It was a unanimous decision to head back to the cabin as the group paid their bill and left.

CHAPTER VI:
HOT CROTCH

"I think I'm gonna hit that sauna downstairs. Been thinking about it all day," said Peter. "Donald, you wanna grab a beer and join me?"

"Yeah, sounds good, dude."

"Enjoy, guys. Let us know how it is," said Terry as she plopped down on the couch next to Kristal.

Downstairs was a large game room with a flat screen TV, sectional couch, small bar, pool table, shower room and sauna.

"Can you believe this place?" said Donald, looking around.

"Yeah, its great wonder how much it costs?"

"Terry looked it up on Zillow. It's a million and a half."

"Holy shit! No surprise there," said Peter as he stood by a small changing area next to the sauna. He began to change, and Donald followed suit. Peter had a lean and muscular body without much fat. Donald assumed he probably played sports at some point.

THE WINTER FOURSOME

"Did you hit that second black diamond this afternoon?" Peter asked as he nonchalantly took off his underwear. His soft cock and balls sprang free. As Peter focused on folding his clothing, Donald quickly took a peek down. His dark pubic hair gave way to his enormous penis that hung down generously past his balls. Donald, feeling a little uneasy, looked away quickly.

"Umm... yeah, yeah I did. That was a tough one huh?"

"Yeah it was definitely tough, but the conditions were shit, ya know? That's what I didn't like. It was all ice out there." Peter grabbed a towel, casually opened the door and walked into the sauna, paying no attention to being naked. Donald removed his underwear, and somewhat awkwardly followed Peter into the sauna. As he walked in, he glanced down at his penis that was practically inverted.

The sauna was not a full-sized one that you would see in a commercial gym or spa. There was really only enough room for four people. Peter and Donald sat facing each other on their towels as they relaxed and sipped their beers.

THE WINTER FOURSOME

"Cold beer and sauna is a great mix, huh?" asked Peter as he took a big gulp.

Donald nodded. "Yep. Great call on that." He said as the awkwardness he was feeling seeped from his voice.

Peter was sitting with his legs spread fairly wide. Donald had a direct line of sight to his crotch but tried as hard as he could to not look directly at it. However, anytime Peter would look away, Donald would look down. He was intrigued by it because Peter's dick was so big. It could hang off the side of the sauna bench with ease. Everyone once in a while, Peter would reposition it. Alternating between laying it across each side, or leaving it in the middle. It seemed like it was just something to do for him. Kind of like playing with a pen or a paper clip during a boring meeting.

Donald wondered if Peter noticed his penis. The heat of the sauna at least helped him relax a bit and it wasn't so contracted like before. But it was still only two inches soft, at best, and rested on top of his balls. Donald obstructed it by positioning his beer can on the bench, only revealing it each time he took a sip. He noticed a couple times when he took a sip, Peter would look down at his crotch. He thought maybe Peter grinned slightly one of the times. *How embarrassing,* Donald thought to himself.

THE WINTER FOURSOME

"Hey, I wanted to say, sorry again for last night. I know Kristal's loud. She's always been like that. I'm sorry if we kept you guys up." Said Peter.

"Oh, dude. Don't even worry about it," said Donald. "It was nothing. Honestly, great for you guys."

"Thanks man. Kristal's so loud. I obviously love it, but would feel horrible if we kept anyone up."

"She certainly is. I laughed so hard at the lodge when she was like, 'You try sticking a ten-inch dick in you!'" Donald laughed. "That was friggin' hilarious."

Peter smiled and nodded, as he looked out the window of the sauna.

Somewhat unexpectedly, Donald said, "must be nice," as he looked down at Peter's crotch.

"What's that?" asked Peter, turning back.

"The, uhh… the ten-inch comment. Must be, uhh, cool."

"Oh, yeah. It's alright," said Peter as he looked down at his own penis for the first time. He picked it up in his hand. This time, Donald watched without hesitation as the conversation was now about Peter's cock.

"Is that thing really ten, dude?" Donald asked, staring directly at it.

"Yeah. Well, not now obviously. But yeah, it can get up there."

"Shit. That's crazy. I'm not even close to that," Donald said with a chuckle.

"It can be kind of a pain sometimes, not gonna lie," Peter said, looking at his penis as he spoke. "Kristal really likes it though."

"Clearly!" said Donald as he took a sip of his beer, revealing his penis.

Peter checked it out in the process. "Hey dude, do you know your measurements?" Donald put his beer down to the side this time, feeling more comfortable with the situation. His penis remained soft, resting comfortably on his sack.

THE WINTER FOURSOME

"Oh me? Umm, yeah I'm like four or five." Donald lied. He knew he was around three and a half, but felt incredibly emasculated in front of Peter.

Peter nodded. "Nice, man. Respectable."

*****

Upstairs, Kristal and Terry chatted on the couch. They had changed into comfortable sweatpants and sweatshirts. Terry curled up with her hair tied in a ponytail, clutching her wine glass.

"Today was so much fun," said Kristal. "You guys are awesome. I'm glad we did this."

"Oh, my God, me too. So nice to get away. I love this house too," Terry said, looking around. The fireplace was crackling in the background.

"Also, I'm beyond mortified about last night. I hope you guys know that was not intentional."

"Oh, stop it, seriously, Kris," said Terry. "You have nothing to be sorry about. Besides, you were having fun, girl!"

THE WINTER FOURSOME

"It was that loud, huh?"

Terry cracked up laughing. "It was indeed that loud! But it's good. You were into it. No shame in that."

"What'd you guys, umm, hear exactly? Just me?" Kristal asked as she tucked her hair behind her ear.

"Oh no, we definitely heard him too. At the end anyway. You were screaming some... high praise."

"Praise?"

Terry lowered her voice and mimicked Kristal. "Oh God, Peter! Oh God, you're so big!" she said in a low volume imitation.

Kristal blushed and covered her face. "Jesus. You heard that, huh?"

Terry nodded. She lovingly clutched her friend's arm. "Don't be embarrassed! I think that's awesome. Seriously, good for you two. And it's nice to hear that about Peter."

Kristal laughed. "No secrets in this house I guess."

Terry stared into the fire for a few seconds before asking Kristal... "you said he's, what, ten inches? Is that really true?"

Kristal nodded as she sipped wine. "When hard, yeah he's pretty big."

"That's crazy. What's that feel like?"

"Well, how big's Donald?" Kristal asked before answering. "Is he big?"

Terry shook her head. "He's average, I guess. I never measured him though," she giggled. "I would guess he's average. It's still nice though."

Kristal smiled. "That's good. Yeah, Peter's a big guy. But it feels so incredible. Just the feeling of being completely filled up. It's super sexy. Like he feels like such a... such a MAN, ya know?"

Terry stared quietly into the fireplace.

"Oh, Terry, you know I didn't mean that to be rude, right? Like of course Donald's a man too. I'm just trying to describe the feeling."

THE WINTER FOURSOME

She smiled at Kristal. "I know. I know. That sounds really great. I'm so happy for you guys, honestly."

"I used to date this guy back in college. I remember he had like the biggest dick. But I didn't like it because he always just kinda stuffed it in ya know? It was impossible to have sex with him."

Kristal nodded. "Yeah they really need to know to be careful when they're big. Peter's super careful and always takes his time. I love it."

"That sounds really nice, actually."

Kristal smiled. "What are they doing down there, anyway? How long can two guys sit in the sauna and talk about the Bucs?"

Terry laughed. "You are drastically underestimating men and football talk."

*****

As the two of them sat there in a moment of silence, Donald couldn't help but stare at Peter's dick. He had never really looked at another man's penis before, nevermind one as substantially large as Peter's. He found himself fascinated with it for some reason.

"You okay there, bud?" Peter asked, noticing Donald was staring.

"Oh, yeah. I'm sorry, man," said Donald looking away. "I'm just impressed, that's all. It's friggin huge."

Peter laughed. "Yeah, it is. You should see this thing when it's hard."

"I can't even imagine, not gonna lie. I'm sittin here trying to picture ten inches," Donald said laughing.

Peter smiled. "See this?" he held up his Bud Light can. "Two of these, maybe a little longer."

"Seriously?" Donald asked, shocked. "That's insane. I can't really believe it, to be honest."

"Gimme a sec, I'll show you." To Donald's complete and utter shock, Peter began squeezing his cock, and wagging it around a bit. He was getting hard in front of Donald! Too surprised to say anything, Donald watched as Peter's dick got bigger and bigger before his eyes. Peter concentrated carefully. In a few short moments, he put his hands by his side, proudly displaying his erection.

Donald was at a loss of words. Next, Peter took the beer can and placed it next to his dick, while steadying it with the other hand. He then moved the beer can up to show how his dick was longer than two of them. Donald stared at the significant length and girth of Peter's hard cock. He guessed it to be close to the thickness of the can as well.

"See what I mean?" asked Peter, finally looking up at Donald. "Whoa, looks like you do," he said as he noticed Donald was rock hard himself.

Donald looked down, not even realizing he had sprouted an erection. "Oh shit, he said. I'm sorry about that."

Peter laughed. "Dude, what are you sorry about? I'm sitting here with a hard-on too. No big deal, man." Peter sat there with his dick pointing straight up, almost to his chest as he looked at Donald's penis. "You sure that's six?"

"Huh? Oh, umm, yeah pretty sure."

"Not tryin' to call you out or anything, just wondering. I don't think it looks like six. Maybe just a hair under that, ya know?"

THE WINTER FOURSOME

"Heh, you may be right, not really sure. Maybe I'll measure it sometime again," Donald said, knowing good and hell well it was maybe four.

"Welp. Alright," Peter said as he stood up, still sporting a raging erection. "I'm gonna shower. There's a couple showers down here. You coming?"

"Umm, yeah, sure man," Donald chugged the rest of his beer and stood up. He felt very uncomfortable leaving the sauna and especially showering with Peter while they both had erections. He followed Peter outside the sauna to the shower room which was directly adjacent. As Peter walked, his large cock swayed left and right. Donald was mesmerized by it.

"Gonna hit the head, see ya in there," said Peter as he went left to the bathroom.

Donald started the shower. He still had a boner and it didn't seem like it was going down anytime soon. He was stunned at how turned on he was by the situation. When Peter walked in, Donald noticed immediately his erection had subsided. He was back to his flaccid state of seven inches.

THE WINTER FOURSOME

The shower was very large and accommodating with four nozzles. The two soaped up as they had casual small talk.

"Dude, you still have a hard-on," said Peter, laughing.

"Fuck, I know," Donald said laughing. "Maybe I'll come have Terry take care of this."

"That'd be nice, huh?"

Donald watched as Peter soaped up his dick and balls. It usually took Donald a couple of seconds to clean his small penis, but Peter had a lot more work to do as he scrubbed all around the giant phallus, making sure to get each nook and cranny. Donald caught himself staring again and made a point to clear his mind as best he could to get his erection to die down. Finally, he regained his control and his penis retracted.

The two men finished showering, got changed, and went to meet the girls upstairs. The experience left Donald shook. He couldn't stop thinking about Peter's big dick. Peter seemed unfazed by any of it. Donald wondered what type of guy he really is. He was about to find out.

*****

THE WINTER FOURSOME

"We thought you guys passed out or something!" said Kristal as Peter and Donald rejoined the women upstairs. "How was it down there?"

"This place is so awesome," said Donald. "There's a four-person sauna, a huge shower, a gym, bar. Everything."

"Why do I smell, like, citrus or something?" Terry asked.

"Shampoo. It's what they had in the shower," Donald replied.

"You guys showered together?" Kristal asked, surprised.

"They have stalls," said Peter. "It's really a huge area down there." Peter intentionally lied to her. Donald was happy about that as he was still unsure of what exactly the two of them just went through. For now, he was relieved it would be a secret.

After dinner, the two couples sat around the fireplace for an hour enjoying each other's company. Kristal sprawled out on the couch in Peter's arms. Terry and Donald shared a love seat.

Terry stretched out and yawned. "I'm exhausted. I think I'm gonna go up."

THE WINTER FOURSOME

"Yeah, me too. Let's hit it. Skiing early tomorrow?" Donald asked as she stood up looking at the other two.

"For sure, bud. See you guys tomorrow," said Peter as he played with Kristal's hair. Donald and Terry went upstairs and closed their bedroom door. They washed up, brushed their teeth and got in bed. In a matter of seconds, Donald was already on top of Terry, kissing her everywhere.

"Whoa, whoa, whoa, where'd you come from?" she asked, giggling as she felt Donald's rock hard dick rubbing against her. Donald didn't say a word, except, "I need this pussy now!" He started to aggressively undress Terry.

"But I just put these on," she said, fake whining. "Okay, okay, okay, easy. Wow, you are really riled up!"

Donald plunged his tongue in Terry's mouth and groped her large breasts. His breath quickened. He moved his mouth to her nipples and devoured them like a Thanksgiving feast. Terry closed her eyes and ran her fingers through his hair. She was getting so wet.

Donald was so turned on from his strange encounter in the sauna, he was like a man on a mission. He quickly pulled Terry's pajama pants down and spread her legs. He didn't even take off her panties, instead pulling them to the side before thrusting his dick into her. Terry gasped at first entry but quickly accommodated. Donald was moving swiftly and was clearly turned on. Terry sensed this wouldn't last too long, so she braced for the inevitable orgasm.

As expected, Donald grunted loudly after only a dozen or so thrusts. He emptied his pent up cum directly into Terry as he moaned and buried his face in her pillow. Terry smiled as she ran her fingertips across Donald's back while he came. She didn't get to cum, unfortunately, but she was happy that Donald felt so good. Donald dismounted Terry and laid next to her, panting as he stared at the ceiling.

"Where did THAT come from?" Terry asked, giggling. "You were really worked up, huh?"

Donald smiled and closed his eyes. "That was fucking awesome!"

"Well, I'm glad you feel better. But how about you wait for me next time?" Terry said with a smile as she went to the bathroom to clean up. Once she returned, she hopped back in bed and cuddled up, holding Donald's hand as they drifted off to sleep.

A couple hours had passed before they were suddenly awakened by the sound of talking and laughing next door. Terry turned to Donald with a look as if to say *here we go again.*

As expected, the bed began creaking. This time was different as, unbeknownst to each other, the two of them were vividly picturing Peter's massive penis penetrating Kristal. It was obvious Kristal was muffling her voice with a pillow or hand. The creaking increased in speed. Peter began to grunt, making no effort to contain his volume.

"You like that?" Peter shouted, loud enough for anyone to hear. "You like that big fucking dick in you?" His powerful, commanding tone was so far from his normal mannerism. It was almost as if Peter was playing a character. The noises continued to echo through the condo as Peter and Kristal had dramatic, intimate intercourse.

"Oh God, oh God, Peter, ohhhhh fuck, fuck, fuck, it's big!" Kristal finally gave up on muffling her voice as she reached orgasm easily. "Yes, yes, yes!"

THE WINTER FOURSOME

Terry turned to Donald and mouthed the words "Oh my God." She looked down and noticed Donald was hard again. This time, he was jerking off. Terry smiled, held his other hand and slipped hers into her panties. She began to feverishly finger herself as Kristal and Peter fucked next door.

The two of them, hands held tightly, masturbating next to each other, both picturing Peter's massive ten-inch dick. Donald couldn't shake the image of him holding his beer can next to it while Terry had to create her own mental imagery from scratch. The fact that the two of them masturbated together, while listening to these two people they knew very well was both weirdly erotic and intimate at the same time.

Donald and Terry had never ventured too far in the bedroom. They normally had fairly vanilla sex. Missionary, oral, and that's about it. Yet here they were, silently masturbating together as Terry's best friend got impaled in the next room.

As Peter's moans and grunts escalated in volume and pace, he was surely nearing orgasm. Terry and Donald both increased their own motions as they too raced towards a mutual climax. Suddenly, the bed next door stopped creaking and Peter let out a very loud grunt as he came.

"Arrrrrghhhhhhh, FUCK!" he shouted as Kristal moaned with him.

Just then, Terry covered her mouth with her hand as she desperately fought back any noise as she came. Donald spat three or four doses of semen all over his belly as he grunted under his breath.

All four of them had cum at relatively the same time, whether or not they knew it. As Terry laid comfortably in the bed, out of breath and in a daze, she pondered what had just happened. She looked over at Donald. He was already asleep, soft penis in hand, cum sliding off his belly onto the sheets below. He was incredibly worked up these past few days. She began to wonder if it was because of Kristal. Maybe he had a crush on her. She was gorgeous, after all. Terry thought to herself, *I wonder if they would ever hookup and I wouldn't be able to tell?* Or maybe it was all because of the sounds of two beautiful people having sex in such close quarters.

She hoped Donald didn't feel embarrassed or less of a man around Peter. But the image of Peter that was plastered in Terry's mind was unmistakably causing arousal in her body that she couldn't shake. She closed her eyes and pictured Peter and Kristal having sex as she drifted off to sleep.

*****

CHAPTER VII:
MORNING AFTER

Unfortunately, the weather the next day did not yield a good day for skiing. It was warm and rainy throughout the day, so the group was forced to hang out inside and pass the time. No one mentioned the previous night when Peter and Kristal's sexcapades were heard throughout the condo. Aside from a few comments here and there, everyone kept the events to themselves.

But Terry couldn't help but notice a difference in Donald. He wasn't his jovial self with her. He was fairly quiet when they woke up and didn't receive any of Terry's not-so-subtle advances. She assumed he was a little embarrassed for jerking off in front of her last night while they listened to Peter and Kristal. But then, she started to think maybe it had something to do with Kristal. Terry thought to herself, *maybe he's not as attracted to me after being around her this weekend.*

Meanwhile, Peter and Kristal were their usual selves. Kristal organized some board games, did some baking, and tried her best to make sure everyone had a fun time indoors. Alcohol was flowing, so it wasn't difficult to get through the day as a group. They even relaxed in the Jacuzzi together a second time.

THE WINTER FOURSOME

"Okay, I have an idea," said Kristal as the group came back inside and were drying off from the soak. They were still in swimsuits, but the two women threw on t-shirts to stay warm. Terry dried her hair off by tilting her head sideways as she listened. The movement of her arms caused her ample breasts to shake.

"We have a table, cups, ping pong balls, and beers. You know what that means?" Kristal asked.

"I haven't played that game in ages," said Donald. "I was really bad back then and I bet I'm even worse now," he joked.

"Ohh, don't be silly. Who cares. Let's play beer pong! Guys versus girls!"

Peter set up the cups and poured beer on one side while Terry did the other. In the process, she had a direct line of sight to his bulge which was incredibly obvious in his tight swim trunks. His soft and thick cock looking rather picturesque in his shorts. He acted like he didn't care that it was visible and couldn't do anything about it anyway.

"Okay, we're all set up. Get over here Donald, let's show these girls how it's done," Peter said. Donald walked over, still in swim trunks. He had kept his shirt on, but Peter opted to take his off. His chiseled abs and broad chest muscles were like eye candy for Terry.

After two games of beer pong, each side had a victory. "We're all tied up, next game is winner take all!" announced Kristal as she geared up to take the first shot.

The last game wasn't even close. The girls beat the guys handily, clearing all cups while the guys had only managed to make three shots.

"That was bad," said Donald as he looked at the table. "That was really bad."

"Yeah, we need some practice over here, looks like," said Peter. "Donald, did you hit a cup the last game?"

Donald shook his head. "No, dude. I suck," he said laughing. "What about a rematch?"

"Yeah, we need a chance at redemption here, girls," added Peter.

"We beat you 2-1! There's no rematch!" said Terry.

THE WINTER FOURSOME

"Okay, okay, sure. How about you make us a deal then? Handicap us or something. Then we play again and try and beat you," Peter proposed.

Kristal and Terry whispered among themselves, coming up with a plan of their own.

"Okay, okay. Boys," started Kristal. "We play again. But this time you guys play naked. Like completely naked, no clothes. And if you beat us while naked? Well, then you win it all."

"How is that a handicap?" asked Donald, confused by the proposal. "Won't you two be distracted and thus have a handicap? Maybe you two should be naked!"

"Very funny. And no chance," said Terry. "You guys get naked or you go home as big fat losers!"

Donald leaned over on the edge of the table, head down, laughing. He turned to Peter. "We doing this?"

Peter shrugged as he started to untie the drawstring of his bathing suit. It appeared he had made up his mind. Donald stood straight and removed his shirt.

THE WINTER FOURSOME

"You know you guys are gonna lose, right?" Donald said, turning to the eagerly waiting women.

Donald looked at Peter, who was smiling, patiently waiting for Donald to pull his shorts down. He shook his head, "Fuck it, here we go," as he pulled down his pants, revealing his shriveled penis sitting atop his balls.

Peter watched Donald disrobe, smiling the entire time. It was now his turn. He didn't make a spectacle out of it. Instead, he casually lowered his bathing suit, stepped out of it, and folded it before placing it on a nearby chair. He stood confidently, penis and balls completely exposed, and took a sip of his beer.

Donald noticed Terry was staring intently at Peter's crotch as he lowered his shorts and let his penis spring free. The look in her eyes was something he had never seen before. She was mesmerized.

Terry desperately tried to play it cool, like she wasn't infatuated with this massive penis in front of her.

"Welp, okay, we have a penis sighting," said Kristal as she laughed, clutching Terry's arm. "Look at these two!"

THE WINTER FOURSOME

Donald stood awkwardly next to Peter. He held his hands up as if to say *oh well* before placing them by his side. Peter stood silent, sipping his beer with his other hand on his hip. His penis hung obscenely low with the head out of view beneath the table.

"Ok, are we ready now?" asked Donald, eager to get the game started. He wound up and fired the ping pong ball directly into a cup on the first try.

"Wow! Looks like somebody's benefiting from a lack of clothing!" Kristal exclaimed.

"Nice shot man," said Peter as he tossed his ball into another cup. Two in a row.

"All of a sudden you guys can play beer pong, huh?" Terry asked as her eyes darted towards Peter's hanging cock. Since they hit two in a row, they got to shoot again. And just like the first time, they each hit another pair of cups. As they high-fived each other, Peter's dick whipped around like a pendulum, nearly taking out the cups on the table.

"Careful Peter, you guys may be up big but you almost gave us a freebie there," Terry giggled.

THE WINTER FOURSOME

The girls finally got a chance to shoot, but both of them missed. "Damn it!" Kristal shouted. "We need to focus over here."

"Told you, it'd be you that has the handicap," Donald teased as he prepared his next shot. All eyes were on Donald as he carefully aimed the ping pong ball. Terry noticed that his cock had grown a bit. She wondered if he was going to get an erection. What would she say if that happened? Would it be best to not acknowledge it? She wondered what Kristal thought of Donald's dick, does she like it even when compared to Peter's?

SPLASH. Donald landed another cup and now the men were up 6-0. "Holy crap, you guys. Terry, maybe we need to be naked. Maybe that's the trick huh?"

"I know, right?" Terry tried her next shot but didn't come close. Peter's dick happened to be right in her line of vision. She could only see about half of it as the table was obstructing the rest. What she saw, however, was impressive. Thick and plump, protruding outwards like an elephant's trunk.

As the score continued to climb out of reach, Donald found himself in a position to win it all. One more cup would guarantee victory. He stood very still, lining up his shot.

"Wait, wait!" Kristal said. She then quickly tore her shirt off revealing her bikini underneath. Then, without hesitation, she untied her string and revealed the biggest, lushest, most beautiful set of breasts Donald had ever seen. Her pink nipples were large and appeared hard. Kristal held them up in her hands looking down, then released them. "We need all the distractions we can get over here!"

Donald couldn't believe his eyes. Kristal was drop dead gorgeous and here she was displaying her amazing breasts for the rest to see. It was too much for Donald. He felt a tingling sensation in his crotch as his brain commanded a fresh supply of blood to be sent there. The arousal was imminent.

"Oh, my God, Kristal, you are friggin' nuts!" Terry said, not believing her teammate was baring it all.

"Cannon alert," said Peter, smiling with a ping pong ball in his hand.

No one seemed to notice or comment on the fact that Donald became hard. It was inevitable one of them would get an erection at some point. Perhaps it was the marginal size difference between his penis when soft versus hard that resulted in no one noticing. Donald braced his legs, wound up, and sunk the final cup.

"Fuck yeah!" shouted Peter as he gave Donald an emphatic high-five.

"Damn," said Kristal. "So much for distracting him." She clutched her boobs.

"Good game, guys," said Peter as he walked over to shake Terry and Kristal's hands, as is a good show of sportsmanship. Terry used every fiber in her being to look at Peter directly in the eyes as he shook her hand and not once look at his glorious cock.

"Whoa, well good afternoon to you too," said Kristal as Donald extended his hand to her. Her eyes were on his hard dick as she smiled at the effect she had.

"Ahh, sorry about that. Shit," said Donald, looking down at his dick. Everyone now glanced down at his hard member.

THE WINTER FOURSOME

"Oh, my God, don't worry about it! I think I'd be slightly upset if you didn't get hard with these out," said Kristal sympathetically.

Terry looked over at the two of them having this conversation with a loathing look. "Donald, oh my God. Put your pants on," said Terry. She put on a fake smile, but the others didn't seem to care about the situation.

"What's the point?" asked Kristal. "Terry, we've seen everything now. I think they stay like this. You won't believe how often Peter and I sit around naked at home."

"It's true," said Peter as he casually leaned against the ping pong table, his dick very much on display. "That's kind of our thing."

Donald was still achingly hard as he too stood next to Peter. The contrast between them was stark. Peter, tall, muscular, and olive with an extremely large soft cock. Donald, short, chubby, and fair with a raging hard on.

"Ok, well, Donald. You should, uh, make that go down or something," said Terry gesturing towards his cock.

"Terry, you know we can't really control these things, right?" Peter asked, defending Donald.

THE WINTER FOURSOME

"Well, you seem to be doing just fine with yours!" said Terry for the first time looking directly at Peter's cock.

"Just depends on the way the wind blows sometimes," said Peter as he looked down at his hanging cock. Peter moved his hands a lot as he spoke, and in doing so his penis would constantly wave back and forth.

"Well, let's hope it doesn't blow your way, Peter. Else we're all in trouble with that thing," said Terry, directly referencing the size of his penis.

Donald was instantly unsettled by the subtle admiration from Terry. He already felt ashamed to be so much smaller than him, and now his wife was openly complimenting the man's cock. He prayed Peter wouldn't get an erection. Donald pictured in his head what it looked like hard from the sauna. It was sure to grab Terry's attention.

Peter was a good sport and laughed it off, careful not to engage further. "Okay, so what do you guys wanna do now? It's getting late, should we pour some wine and start dinner?"

THE WINTER FOURSOME

"I'm good with that," said Kristal. "A little group nude cooking session?"

"I'll go bikini, how's that?" asked Terry as she removed her shirt. She wasn't quite as brazen as her friend.

"Completely cool! And sexy!" Kristal exclaimed.

The group muddled about the kitchen preparing dinner. It was a unique sight to be seen as Peter and Donald, both completely naked, moved about the kitchen. Donald sported an erection the entire time, and Peter remained completely soft. Terry was less and less subtle as she continued to admire Peter's penis. They stood at either side of the kitchen island together, facing one another, cutting up vegetables.

Peter leaned across the island to get a carrot that rolled away. In the process, his penis ended up on the counter in front of him, instead of tucked away below. Peter continued to cut the vegetables, with it in plain sight, and his balls rested below.

"Oh, um, Peter, your... your ummm... " Terry said as she pointed at his cock. She guessed it to be at least six or even inches long and already thicker than Donald's in its flaccid state.

THE WINTER FOURSOME

"Oh... oops," he said, stepping back a bit to let it fall down below again. He held up the knife he was using. "That wouldn't have been good huh?"

"I imagine that can get in the way from time to time," Terry joked.

Donald, with his back to both of them, pretended to not hear the conversation happening. But Kristal certainly did.

"You guys have no idea. Sometimes I need to literally tell Peter to get his dick out of the way!"

Terry cracked up laughing. "Really? Like when?"

"Okay, so last summer we went down to the Cape and rented bikes. And Peter, you were wearing those wicked short shorts. You bought them the day before in Provincetown, remember? So he gets on the bike and we're cruising around, whatever, enjoying the day. And we stop at this dock. There were like a bunch of people around us. And I look over and he's just looking at the water, completely unaware that his friggin' dick is, like, peaking out. Out of his shorts! Just chilling in the damn breeze!"

THE WINTER FOURSOME

Terry was dying laughing. She covered her mouth with her hand.

"I'm like, Peter, put your fuckin' dick back in your pants, there's kids around here! The thing is so big, it just had nowhere to go." Kristal continued, with her loud laugh echoing.

The only one not laughing was Donald. He patiently listened to the story, glancing down at Peter's dick from time to time. He decided he didn't like hearing Terry being so infatuated with Peter's cock.

But hearing and experiencing were two different things. The truth was he was incredibly aroused by it all. He felt he couldn't fully satisfy Terry. But she still loved him. He wanted her to enjoy herself, and if that meant being interested in another man's penis, then so be it. He looked down at his unrelenting still hard cock and prayed it would go down. Unfortunately, he had a sinking feeling there was only one way it was going away.

"That is seriously so funny," said Terry. "Peter, did you really not notice it?"

THE WINTER FOURSOME

"No clue. Like she said, I was taking in the view. Only problem was I guess others were taking in the view too," he joked.

"Who wouldn't?" asked Kristal. She sauntered over to Peter and put her arms around his broad shoulders. She stood on her tippy toes, pressing her large breasts against him, and kissed him on the cheek. "I love your big ol' dick, Peter."

"Aww, you guys," said Terry as she focused on her vegetable cutting again. "So sweet."

"Ok. Salad is ready. Chicken's in. We are looking good, guys!" Kristal announced as she looked around the kitchen, stopping at Donald. He was still leaning against the counter sipping a glass of wine.

"Donald, tell me. Is this normal for you?" She pointed towards his hard penis. Precum oozed from the tip. "You've been hard basically since the beer pong game."

Donald blushed. "I can assure you this is most certainly not normal." He wiped off some of the excess precum.

"You can have your moments," added Terry as she smacked on some crackers. "Remember on our honeymoon the night we stayed in that treehouse thing? You were hard a lot that night."

"Wow, very specific memory," Kristal laughed.

"Yeah, you have a great boner memory huh?" added Peter.

"Yeah, I don't know why I remembered that of all the things we did on that trip!" Terry giggled.

The conversation lulled a bit as everyone had a good laugh. But the attention remained on Donald with his erection.

"So, do you need to, uhh, take care of that? Or what?" Kristal asked. Donald smiled. "I think so, if we're being honest here. I'm sorry, guys. I'll go upstairs quickly and get rid of it."

"Why not here, man?" Peter asked. "We don't care, really. Kristal and I are cool about this kinda stuff," he said as he pointed to his penis and then her breasts.

"Terry, would you please go jerk your husband off? For crying out loud, look at this poor man," Kristal pleaded.

THE WINTER FOURSOME

Terry cracked up laughing, hesitantly. She looked at Donald, who had a somewhat excited look on his face, like a dog waiting to catch some food that gets dropped.

"Seriously?" she asked.

"Of course! Look at him. He needs help, Terry!"

Terry stared at Donald's penis. "Okay, okay, get over here honey."

Donald walked over to Terry, who was now seated at the kitchen island stool. Donald stood next to her as she took hold of his aching cock. She kissed him gently on the cheek before lazily stroking it. Donald felt relief almost immediately as Terry's soft hand took hold of him.

"How's that feel?" Kristal asked as she watched the handjob unfold. Kristal sat next to Terry at the island, while Peter remained standing across the kitchen.

Donald didn't respond, but instead he grabbed Terry's hand in a panic, holding it steady.

"You okay?" she asked.

THE WINTER FOURSOME

"Yeah, yeah, I'm good. I just thought I was about to lose it there for a second," Donald said as he regained his composure.

Kristal looked at Peter, smiling. She thought it was cute Donald was trying to hold back after a few seconds. She knew this was never an issue with Peter.

Terry continued stroking him, slower this time, making sure not to rush things. Donald held his hands tightly behind his back as he felt his pleasure mount quickly. He looked at Kristal's boobs which were pressed firmly together as she sat with her hands in her lap. She was gorgeous. Terry's little hands raced up and down his cock. It was useless to fight the urge. He was going to cum.

"Fuck," Donald said calmy as he fired a thick blast of ejaculate directly onto Terry's chest. She jumped back a bit, not expecting his orgasm so soon.

"Oh!" she cried out.

Donald expelled two more shots of his load onto her chest and the floor beneath them. The third and fourth were smaller and dribbled out onto Terry's hand. She decreased her pace as Donald shuttered with sensitivity.

THE WINTER FOURSOME

He finally stepped back, done and spent. "Okay, okay. That's good. Wow. Fuck that felt good. Thanks, babe."

"Of course!" Terry said sweetly as she examined the semen covering her hand and chest. "You had a lot, huh?"

Donald nodded, unable to speak. He caught his breath as he looked around at the mess he created. "I'll take care of this. Sorry, guys."

His post-nut clarity moment caused him to feel extremely embarrassed about what just happened. He looked over at Peter who calmly watched, sipping his drink. Donald peeked at his cock which seemed to have grown a bit.

"That was hot, guys!" said Kristal as she started setting up for dinner. "Donald, you must feel relieved."

"I am very. Felt awesome. Let's eat."

CHAPTER VIII:
DINNER THEATER

The group sat at the end of the large 12-seat dining room table. Everyone had put their clothes back on. The feeling of nudity had become strangely comfortable for Donald, even though this was never anything he and Terry had explored before. Terry couldn't help but to think about what she'd witnessed, now covered by Peter's pants.

"So guys," said Kristal as Terry quickly snapped out of her trance. "If you make a baby this weekend, will you name it after the mountain?"

Terry laughed. "I don't think so. I'm not sure Sunday River is a good name for a baby."

"Sounds more like a porn name," joked Donald.

"Did you know if you take your pet's name and the street you grew up on, that's your porn name? Mine's Daisy Crestivew," Kristal announced.

"That's actually a good one. Mine would be Spot 5th," Terry said. "Not a great one, guys."

THE WINTER FOURSOME

"I had a fish named Phyllis. So, I guess I am Phyllis Academy," said Donald. Everyone cracked up. "What would you be, Peter?"

Peter didn't respond, instead he looked at Kristal with a slight grin on his face. "You wanna tell them?" he asked.

"What?" asked Terry.

"Guys, Peter sort of . . . already has a porn name."

"What do you mean?" asked Donald. "You've done porn?"

Peter nodded. "Couple years back I did some modeling. It was for a gay porn site. Just pictures and stuff. Nothing too crazy. But I met this lady there who was running a site of her own. Kinda niche stuff. She asked if I wanted to do a couple videos."

"You did porn videos?" Terry asked, nearly falling out of her chair.

Peter smiled. "A couple, yes. Again, guys. It was weird stuff. Kinda specific."

"Okay, like what?"

THE WINTER FOURSOME

"Well, basically I would be with a group of girls. Everyone's wearing clothes except me. And the girls would kind of talk about me and laugh at me, just be kinda playful. Eventually one of them would jerk me off. And that's kind of it."

"So handjob porn?" asked Donald. "That's not really niche."

"No, you guys the girls literally don't get naked," said Kristal. "They're all clothed. And they jerk him off onto their clothes and stuff. I think they call it cfnm porn."

"That's so crazy. How many videos did you do?" Terry asked, leaning in excitedly.

"There are four of them online. I shot more, but I never saw them. They could be out there somewhere. I'm not sure."

"What was your name?"

Peter smiled as he took a bite of salad. He held up one finger indicating to wait until he was done chewing. "Rosco Slim."

THE WINTER FOURSOME

Everyone burst out laughing. "Rosco Slim?" Donald said. "What the hell does that mean?"

Peter laughed and took a sip of wine. "The lady thought I looked like her ex boyfriend named Rosco. And I was a lot skinnier back then, not a lot of muscle. Hence, 'slim.' I don't know you guys, it was weird."

"That's hilarious. I never knew this about you, Peter. You're a legit porn star!" said Terry.

He dismissed the claim. "No, no, you guys. I'm not a star. I don't do it anymore. Just a one time thing."

"I wanna see them," said Terry. "Can we see the videos?"

Donald frowned at her. Jealousy spiked as he imagined Terry watching the videos and marveling at Peter's penis. But deep down, he wanted to see them too. In fact, he kind of wanted Terry to watch.

"If you guys want," Peter said, laughing. "I'm telling you, they're not that great. Super cheesy."

Kristal was already on her phone, typing feverishly. "I'll get them. I know which one I want to show them."

THE WINTER FOURSOME

"Oh God, Kris. Not the swimming lessons one."

She smiled as she turned her phone sideways and propped it up so everyone could see. Terry leaned in to get a good look. Peter continued to eat his dinner while everyone else watched.

On the screen Peter was wearing a red speedo. In front of him were three girls. Two blonde, one brunette. They were all wearing one piece bathing suits. Peter appeared to be teaching them swimming lessons. The trio laughed over the cheesy dialogue in the video.

The focus of the video was almost exclusively on Peter. There were multiple close up shots of his bulge under the speedo. His thick penis could barely be contained. It ran underneath the suit towards his hip.

"Your bathing suit's a little small, huh?" asked Terry, looking up at Peter.

Peter glanced at the phone while chewing his dinner. "It was intentional."

"Okay, hold on. Let me fast forward through all this," said Kristal as she slid her finger along the track bar. Terry didn't say anything even though she wanted to watch

THE WINTER FOURSOME

every second of the video. "Here," she said, propping the phone up again.

Peter sat in a beach chair as the girls crowded around him. One of them had their hands on his cock while another held his balls. The one jerking him off could easily use two hands as she stroked him up and down. Kristal closely observed both Terry and Donald's reaction as they watched the movie. Peter's deep grunting from the video filled the room.

"Holy shit," said Terry softly as the camera zoomed in on Peter's cock. She looked up at Peter, bewildered.

Kristal proudly agreed. "Right?" she said.

"That's insane," Terry again said, not shy about voicing her admiration.

Donald sat mostly quiet watching the film. He was definitely aroused watching it. He was still reluctant to admit that he wanted the video to turn on Terry too.

He glanced at her to gauge her interest. She was enthralled, eyes wide open, mouth dropped. Donald could tell she was aroused. He liked that. But at the same time it was because of a man who wasn't him. A man

THE WINTER FOURSOME

sitting across from them all in the flesh. Donald was rock hard under his shorts again.

"Okay, okay, watch!" said Kristal. In the video, the camera panned out so that all three women were visible. Peter's head tilted back and he closed his eyes. He grunted loudly as a massive thick, white, rope of cum launched out of his cock and into the air. It went so high that it was completely out of frame. Another blast followed as thick and creamy ejaculate landed in one of the girls' hair.

"Damn!" shouted Terry, hands on her cheeks, mouth dropped to the floor. Peter continued moaning and grunting as he fired three more thick blasts. The girl jerking him off aimed one at each of the girls, soaking them all.

"Oh my God," Terry continued. "This is crazy!"

Terry lost count of how many times Peter's cock spasmed. His orgasm was impressive in both duration and volume. She never recalled a time Donald came that much. The tingling sensation between her legs had transformed into a full blown soaking wet arousal. She fidgeted in her seat, trying to stimulate herself even if just slightly.

THE WINTER FOURSOME

Peter's cock spat out a couple more dribbles of cum on its own with no one jerking it as the camera zoomed in to catch the final moments. There was nothing but his towering cock and dripping cum in the frame now.

"Whoa," said Terry as the movie came to an end.

Kristal put her phone down and looked at Terry, who was in shock. "See? Crazy right?" she asked.

Terry nodded and sipped her wine. She glanced at Peter. "That was really cool, Peter. You, uhh... you definitely put on a show. How did you, like, cum that much? Do they give you something?"

Peter shook his head. "I just can. I always have. The lady who got me into this said that was the reason she wanted me for the films."

"My little porn star," said Kristal as she lovingly patted his back.

"Little? Not quite, Kris," said Terry as she picked up her fork and resumed eating her dinner.

After dinner, the group hung out for a bit before turning in. It was a long day and everyone had plenty to drink.

THE WINTER FOURSOME

Donald fell asleep almost immediately, and Terry could hear him snoring softly next to her. She lay in bed, wide awake, unable to shake the image from her head of Peter in the video.

Then she heard the inevitable sounds of Kristal and Peter having sex, like they did every night. This time Terry had a vivid, accurate mental image to pair with the sounds she heard.

She checked to make sure Donald was still asleep before slipping her hand in her panties and massaging her clit. She dreamed of Peter's big cock and listened intently as he slammed it into Kristal in the nex troom. The combination of Kristal's moans with Peter's grunts was overcoming her. Terry rubbed herself in a slow but determined motion as her wetness increased rapidly.

"Oh God! Yes, fuck, fuck, fuck, oh my God Peter," Kristal moaned in ecstacy.

"You like this? You like this big dick?"

"It's so big. Oh my God. Oh! Fuck! God it's big!" she shouted back.

THE WINTER FOURSOME

Terry was close to coming, but she was not quite there yet. She continued rhythmically masturbating as she listened. She spread her legs further and plunged her middle finger inside deep. Her ecstasy grew.

Suddenly, she heard a loud moan from Kristal and a deep grunt from Peter. They were certainly coming together. Peter grunted repeatedly as Terry pictured how much cum he was probably unloading on her. She continued to touch herself as Donald snored next to her.

It was then silent as she heard Kristal and Peter laughing. She wondered if they were laughing at how much cum was probably everywhere or if it was just typical after-sex laughter. She kept masturbating to her mental imagery. As silence fell upon the house, she realized she was the only one up now. But she was still painfully horny and desperately needed to come.

Terry reached for her phone and opened up a private browser. In the search box, she typed "Rosco Slim." Sure enough, four videos came up. She clicked the swimming lesson one and fast forwarded to the cumshot. As she watched Peter's penis erupt all over the girls, she herself erupted in a deep and powerful orgasm. She closed her lips tightly to not make a loud noise as pleasure took her entire body hostage. The video was over, but her orgasm continued to ripple. Finally, relief.

She put her phone down, closed her eyes, and rode out the rest of her pleasure. Donald was still fast asleep next to her.

Once it was over, she felt elation and guilt at the same time. She just masturbated to the man in the other room again. And even as she drifted off to sleep, she still couldn't get the image of Peter out of her head.

THE WINTER FOURSOME

CHAPTER IX:
EARLY BIRD

Donald woke to the sound of everyone talking downstairs. He glanced at the clock. 10:17 am. He was immediately angry with himself for sleeping so late because he wanted to get up and get on the mountain early. Conditions were supposed to be excellent, as the rain had turned to snow overnight. He brushed his teeth and got dressed in long johns and underlayers. He walked downstairs to find Terry, Kristal, and Peter sitting around the kitchen island drinking coffee.

"Hey, babe," said Terry with a smile as Donald emerged. Peter grabbed a cup and poured Donald some coffee. Peter's hair was messed up and his face was flush. He was wearing his underlayer clothing as well but appeared to have already gone skiing.

"Did you do a run?" Donald asked as he sipped his coffee.

"Yep. Started around 6:00 am, when the west lift opened. Just got back. It's really nice out there."

"I'm gonna go after this. Anyone else?"

THE WINTER FOURSOME

Terry and Kristal were not in any way ready to go skiing. Kristal looked hungover, and Terry was not that much of a skier anyway.

"I'm good," Kristal said.

Terry nodded. "Me too. You go though. Don't let us stop you. By the way, this coffee is amazing," she said as she poured another cup. "What is it?"

"Some Costa Rican stuff. It was here when we showed up," Peter replied.

The group seemed content to carry on as if nothing strange had happened yesterday. The naked beer pong, the handjob, and watching Peter in a porn video were all things that Terry and Donald had never dreamed of doing with friends. But Peter and Kristal had such a carefree way of making everything seem normal.

"Whoops, looks like I went a little overboard on the cream," Peter said as he poured out his coffee and tried again.

"What's with you and cream overload?" Kristal asked, winking.

THE WINTER FOURSOME

Donald smiled and shook his head. "Gross. Okay, thanks for the coffee. But I'm burning daylight here." Donald rose to his feet to get his ski clothes on. He kissed Terry on the cheek. "I'll see you guys after lunch."

"Have fun, man. I may see you out there later. Gonna chill for a bit," Peter said.
*****

Terry, Kristal, and Peter sat around the large and comfortable living room chatting while Donald hit the slopes. Terry couldn't help but think about her masturbation session last night. How she listened to these two have sex while she fingered herself furiously.

Terry found herself checking out Peter's bulge over and over again, basically at any chance she could get. He sat somewhat slouched on the couch looking at his phone. She could see the outline of it in his tight long johns. Her conversation with Kristal helped keep her gaze from being noticed.

"And the problem is that they don't have the market share needed to get more clients. Because they're not investing in the right areas, you know? It's a catch-22. And our group is constantly dealing with it," said Terry. She and

THE WINTER FOURSOME

Kristal were in the same industry but worked for different companies.

"So frustrating," said Kristal. "It's not an easy industry, huh?"

Terry shook her head and crossed her legs. She kicked her foot mindlessly as the conversation halted a bit. Then, she broke the silence.

"So, Peter," she said as she got his attention. "Do you still do your modeling? You said that's how you got into everything last night, right?"

"Naw," Peter said as he sat upright on the couch. "Different times. I'm kinda past that now. It was fun though."

"I'm sure it was," Terry smiled.

"No, no, the modeling," Peter laughed. "But yeah, that other stuff was fun too."

"Are you ever worried someone's gonna see it? Like family, friends, or an employer?"

THE WINTER FOURSOME

"We talk about that all the time, don't we?" Kristal asked, looking at Peter.

He nodded. "I do think about it. But what can you do? It's out there, it's part of me, and I have to just own it."

"That's a good mindset," said Terry. "You should be proud of it, honestly."

"Yeah?" asked Peter.

"Of course! You've got a big dick. You just want to share it with the world, don't you?"

The group laughed. "It really is amazing, hun," said Kristal. She turned to Terry. "I tell him all the time how in love I am with that thing."

"You tell the whole condo that too," Terri joked. Peter laughed the hardest at that joke. They all thought back to Kristal's appreciation of the size of Peter's penis the night before.

"What'd you guys say it was, ten inches? That's freakin crazy. When I saw it, I was like 'what the fuck?'"

"Right?!" Kristal agreed.

THE WINTER FOURSOME

"So, yesterday," Terry started laughing as she recalled her story. "Yesterday, when you pulled your pants down and just stood there. The thing was hanging, like so low. My jaw dropped. To the floor. I was shocked."

"Yup. Me too, every time. Even still," Kristal said smiling at Peter. "It's so impressive."

After a brief period of silence, Kristal turned back to Peter. "Peter, how's it looking today?"

"Excuse me?"

"Your dick. How does it look today? I think we should let him free for a bit."

Peter nodded towards Terry. "You sure?"

"Why not?" Terry asked, stepping in. "We already saw it. I actually kinda want to see it again."

"Umm... shouldn't we wait until Donald gets back?" Peter asked.

"Donald's skiing. We'll be lucky if he comes back by next Tuesday," joked Terry. "But seriously, I friggin' jerked him off in front of you guys yesterday. I'm not sure this is such a big deal anymore."

"She's got a good point. Peter?"

Peter shrugged and stood up. First he removed his socks before sliding his long johns off. Underneath, he wore tight black compression shorts. His large bulge was clearly visible. Terry's eyes were wide as she anticipated the reveal. Kristal watched Terry's reaction with the same excitement. She loved seeing another woman be impressed with Peter.

Without much hesitation, Peter peeled off his compression shorts and let his long, heavy cock free from its confines. He stood there for a moment, holding his shirt up so the girls could see.

"Holy fuck," Terry said, looking between Kristal and Peter. "That's so big."

Peter looked down at it. He spotted a small black strand of fabric from the compression shorts and pulled it off his sack.

"Babe, hold it up a little, would you?"

THE WINTER FOURSOME

Peter picked up his shaft and held it off to the side, allowing the women to see his large balls.

"Look how friggin' huge those are," Kristal said laughing. "Every time I see them, I can't believe it."

Peter held his shirt up between his chest and chin so he could use his other hand to gently lift his balls. He rolled them around in his hand, displaying their immense volume and weight.

"Damn," Terry uttered to no one in particular.

"Ok, ok, are we good, ladies?" Peter asked, his eyes searching for an answer.

"I kinda wanna see it hard," said Terry, eager to keep the strip show going. Strangely enough, she turned to Kristal with her proposition, as if Kristal was in charge of whether or not Peter continued. "Is that weird?"

"Umm, no," Kristal laughed. "Who wouldn't want to see him hard?"

Kristal stood up and walked over to Peter. She lifted his shirt up over his head so he was completely naked. "Let's see what we can muster up here," she announced as she took hold of his massive penis. "Actually, let's sit down. That will be a lot easier."

Peter sat on the couch, positioned between Kristal and Terry. Terry's eyes were glued to his crotch. She sat with her legs crossed, hands neatly wrapped around her coffee cup as she settled in for a show.

"You sure about this? I feel bad with Donald not being here," said Peter as Kristal casually played with his dick.

"Oh no, don't be. Donald would be all about this. He's a hornball."

"Oh, we know. He's the boner king," said Kristal, giggling. "Speaking of boners. Look who's already playing along."

Peter's dick had begun to take shape, expanding significantly in Kristal's small hand. The thick veins became more and more pronounced as the shaft expanded in length and girth. Kristal's hand ran up and down in long, consistent strokes, squeezing out precum each trip it made to his head.

Soon, Peter had achieved a full erection. Kristal's fingers couldn't touch each other due to its girth. His dick was so long, in fact, that it could have reached his xiphoid process if she angled it back that way.

"God, you guys," said Terry, mesmerized by what she saw in front of her. "This is, like, the craziest thing I've ever seen in person."

"Wait 'til he cums," said Kristal, smiling. "No, like seriously, wait 'til you see him cum."

"I saw in the movie! Crazy…"

Peter put his hands behind his head and leaned back, enjoying the handjob. Kristal used both hands as she gritted her teeth and focused hard on her work.

Peter kept looking at Terry, who he knew had not broken her gaze since he initially took his pants off. Her eyes were filled with lust and desire. There was no doubt she was physically beautiful, but Peter was also deeply attracted to her kind demeanor and joyful attitude. Not to mention her apparent preoccupation with his cock.

"Mmmmmm," said Peter as he closed his eyes and leaned back even further. Terry's eyes widened as she looked at Kristal. "Coming soon?"

THE WINTER FOURSOME

"I think so," she responded.

"I could, if you guys want. Or not. Your call," Peter responded, opening his eyes.

"Oh my god, really? How is that possible?" Terry asked, shocked. Donald could never hold out for the most part. They usually had sex for no more than five minutes. Terry normally insisted on foreplay if she wanted to get off first, or at all.

"Years of practice. And it helps to have a great partner too," Peter said as he lovingly caressed Kristal's back.

"I think you should cum," said Kristal as she doubled down on his dick and really started grinding both of her hands. "You think it'll be like last night?"

"Yes," Peter said as he looked into Terry's beautiful eyes, which were glued to his cock. She was the reason Peter was so aroused at the moment. He loved when women stared at it. He pictured Donald's small penis and questioned if Terry was missing something in her life. Her obsession with staring at him led him to believe that was true.

THE WINTER FOURSOME

"Okay, well we don't really have anything to contain the blast," Kristal said with a huge smile as she looked around the room.

"What do you need? You want me to get a towel?" Terry asked, eager to help.

"No," Kristal laughed. "He'd shoot right past it. Umm... here, why don't I just aim you up like this. This ceiling is like fifteen feet high. It'll just fall back down onto you."

"Kris, it's gonna go everywhere. That's not gonna work," he warned as she continued working.

"Here," Terry said as she put her coffee cup down and held out her hands together, forming a little basket. "I'll try to catch it?"

Peter looked at her little hands and laughed. "You have no idea how much I cum."

The moment arrived as Peter started moaning. "Oh God. Keep going. Keep going. Fuck. Shit. Okay . . . here we go."

Peter gestured for Terry to come closer, which she did almost immediately. She placed her hands at the tip of Peter's dick while Kristal angled it down into them. The first moment her hands made contact with his dick head, a wave of arousal flew through Terry's body, culminating in her wet pussy. She stared at a strand of precum that connected her thumb and his dick.

"Arggghhhhhhhh!" Peter shouted loudly, just like the few nights previously. It was intense to hear his groaning up close and in person.

Peter fired a massive rocket of cum directly into Terry's outstretched hands. It was so strong it ricocheted back onto Peter's stomach. Terry screamed at the sheer intensity of it. He kept cumming as two more equally strong blasts coated her hands and his stomach.

"Oh my God, Peter!" Terry screamed as she watched him unload into her hands.

"Fuuuuuuccckkk!!! Ahhhhhh!!" screamed Peter as he lifted his midsection into the air and watched another massive load spray past Terry's hands and onto the floor at least two feet away.

"Whoa!" Terry shouted as she watched how far he shot.

"Oh God, babe," Kristal said as she continued to stroke him, her voice peaking in arousal. Peter stretched his legs out and kept cumming. Terry's hands were full; there was no more room. She pulled them back, careful not to spill any, and watched Kristal jerk Peter off directly up, as originally planned. He fired two weaker blasts up in the air, all landing down on his chest. Kristal and Terry watched as if they were watching a fireworks display. Peter grunted over and over again as he reached the final blast of cum.

He leaned back, eyes closed and out of breath. Kristal held his dick in one hand and rested her other hand on her breasts. Terry, still holding his initial load, looked around the room, completely in shock as to how much this man just came in front of her.

"This is insane. You're unbelievable!" she said.

"Look how thick it is too," Kristal said as she played with his cum in her hand. "I love the consistency."

Terry looked down at her own sample as his semen completely filled her cupped hands. She admired the color, texture, and smell. The smell of his thick cum was intoxicating, but she couldn't think of an easy way to explain tasting it. All she could think about was wanting to feel it oozing down her throat. She couldn't help but compare it with Donald's load, which was normally two or three spurts and rather unimpressive.

"How many times did you cum?" Terry asked.

Peter opened his eyes, looking confused. "Once, I'm pretty sure," he laughed.

Terry laughed too. "No, like how many shots was that?"

"Eight." said Kristal, answering for him. "We've counted. It's almost always eight."

"Holy shit," Terry said looking back down at her hands. "That's really incredible. I gotta say… I'm super impressed, Peter."

"Well, thanks Terry. You were a great helper today," he said as he clutched her shoulder. His big, strong hands on her body were enough to send a quiver straight to her vagina, which was already a ticking time bomb. She instinctively recoiled back upon contact. Peter took it as a sign to retreat, but in reality she didn't want to set anything off.

"Welp. I gotta clean this up, huh?" Peter said as he looked around the room. A long, unbroken streak of his cum laid out across the floor in front of him. Kristal's hands were caked in it, and it was dripping all over Peter's chest and stomach. Terry watched his chiseled abs contract in and out as he breathed, covered in his own jizz.

"Don't move. Let me get you a towel so you don't make more of a mess," said Kristal as she went upstairs.

Peter and Terry were left on the couch. "So, how are things going?" Peter asked before cracking up. Terry burst out laughing, savoring the shared moment. Peter was completely naked, covered in his own cum, while Terry held her hands tightly together, carefully cradling a puddle of cum.

"Oh my god, my stomach hurts from laughing. Stop making me laugh," she said. "Look at how much there is. Just look around. How is this possible from one human being?"

"What, you mean Donald doesn't spray you like a firehose?" he joked.

Peter calmed and quieted down. Terry giggled as she glanced at Peter's soft penis. "It goes to your thigh."

"Hmm?" Peter looked back at Terry.

THE WINTER FOURSOME

"Your penis. It's hanging, "she pointed out.

"Oh. Well, yeah, he's just taking a quick nap right now. He's sleepy." Peter playfully petted his penis as if it were a sleeping dog.

Terry cracked up. "You're hilarious."

Kristal came downstairs carrying a large, gray towel. She tossed it at Peter, who proceeded to wipe his chest down. "It's gray so hopefully we don't get dinged on any stains," she joked.

Peter stood up to begin cleaning the floor.

"Are you forgetting something?" Terry asked as she held out her hands.

"Oh my god, shit. Sorry, Terry." Peter held out the towel, allowing Terry to dump his cum into it. Peter got on his hands and knees to wipe up his long shot from the floor. When he was done, he sat back down opposite the girls, giving them some space and a view. Terry took advantage of the opportunity.

THE WINTER FOURSOME

"Okay. I was already in need of a shower after skiing, and now I'm a mess. I'm gonna jump in. Be down in a bit, guys," Peter said as he walked directly in front of the girls and headed upstairs, his heavy penis swaying back and forth the whole time.

"Peter, honey? No clothes when you come down, please?"

Kristal turned back towards Terry once he was out of sight. "Well, that was fun," she said as both women laughed. Terry clutched her arm as she leaned forward in her seat.

"Kristal, can I just say? Wow. That's all. Just wow."

"What? His dick? Or the buckets of cum?"

"Both! I've never seen anything like it. I can't believe it, honestly."

"He really is amazing with what God gave him. And let me tell ya, God gave him some gifts, alright," Kristal said.

"Ok, so in two days we've each jerked our significant other's off in front of each other. Played naked beer pong. And had loud and raucous sex in close confines. What else is there to do?" Terry joked.

THE WINTER FOURSOME

"We're doing it all, sister!" Kristal exclaimed with a high five.

"Can I just say, I've...we've never done anything like this before. Like, sometimes we're a little goofy at home together. Like one night we made dinner naked, just for fun. But other people? No, never. Yesterday was a complete first time for that."

"It's so fun though, right? I'd be lying if I said we were strangers to this too. We're super kinky, Terry. Like, we've gone to sex parties and stuff."

"Sex parties? Oh, my god, never. I can't imagine actually cheating on Donald."

"No, no, no," said Kristal. "We never cheat. It's all consensual with everyone involved. All in good fun. You'd like it, I think."

"So, you see other women have sex with Peter?"

Kristal nodded. "And I sleep with other men too. We do it for the thrill, and it's incredibly arousing. Like, to sit there and watch another woman try and uhh, make him fit," Kristal said as she turned beet red. "It's so hot, Terry."

THE WINTER FOURSOME

Terry couldn't help but feel incredibly aroused by Peter naked, just as she got aroused listening to the couple have sex the night before. She didn't dare mention she masturbated to their sounds last night or the night before with Donald. She may never mention it. But her deep interest in it was unmistakable.

"Is he really just gonna be naked when he comes down? Like yesterday?"

"Mmm hmm. As long as you're okay with it, and I think you are." Kristal winked.

Terry thought about it for a moment before grinning and smiling. "I guess I wouldn't mind," she teased. Terry looked up at the top of the stairs and listened for the shower running. Peter was still in there. She leaned in close to Kristal and lowered her voice to a whisper. "How on Earth do you guys have sex?"

Kristal laughed. She too looked up the stairs to make sure the coast was clear. "It wasn't easy at first. Sometimes, it still isn't easy. He's huge, Terry. Like the biggest dick I've ever seen, period."

THE WINTER FOURSOME

"No shit! I couldn't believe it when I saw it in the video and then today. My, oh my."

"You have to go slow. Like really slow. You know the phrase 'just the tip'? Yeah, that's us. Literally us every time," Kristal said as she sat back and crossed her legs. "But once it's in... pure joy."

Terry couldn't imagine. Donald's length was less than half of Peter's, and considerably less girthy too. "I'm sure it is. I can hear you nightly."

"Oh God," Kristal buried her face in her hands. "I'm so loud. I'm sorry. I can't help it. He feels so good. Plus, I'm just a natural screamer anyway."

"For sure!" exlcaimed Terry. "It's all good though."

Just then, Peter descended from the stairs, completely naked. The allure of his fresh out the shower mountain man scent, and his long penis stole the show. His abs still glistening with beads of water from the shower. Both women watched. His long penis stole the show instantly with its rhythmic bouncing. He quietly took his seat in the same spot, put his legs up on the coffee table, and crossed his arms. "Is this what you had in mind?"

THE WINTER FOURSOME

"Yes," Terry answered.

Peter raised his eyebrows. "Well, okay then Terry," he laughed. "Your wish is my command!"

The three of them spent the afternoon hanging around the house, watching TV and chatting. Terry decided she was staying put with Peter's cock out and about. Besides, she'd had only limited interest to begin with in meeting Donald for a few runs. She couldn't wait to see Donald's face when he walked in. She hoped he wouldn't be upset. She hoped he would want to join in for some more group fun.

"I still can't believe you did porn, Peter," said Terry. "I mean, I can, but it's still just crazy to me."

"Thanks. Yeah, it was definitely an experience," Peter said as he picked up his penis, mindlessly. "So guys, I've been sitting here naked. When are the two of you gonna join the fun?"

Terry hesitated, and Peter realized his advance might be inappropriate. "Terry, shit. I'm sorry. I didn't mean to make you uncomfortable. You know that. I mean my beautiful girlfriend over here, who just so happens to be

THE WINTER FOURSOME

quite the exhibitionist at home, seems like she is ready for some action."

"Hey! I showed my boobs yesterday. For a while!"

Peter wagged his penis teasingly. "Krissstalllll, please get naked," he said in a high-pitched squeal. Terry cracked up. "Kristal, I think it wants to see you."

"Fine. But only for him," she said as she pointed to Peter's cock. "Because it's him I really care about. The rest? Meh, take it or leave it."

"Love you too, sweetie."

Kristal stood up and cheerily removed her shirt in a kind of slow striptease motion. Her gorgeous breasts emerged, still held in place by her red lace bra. Kristal was in great shape, slim and tight. Despite her petite frame, her large breasts were magnificently prominent. She squeezed them together with her elbows and sexily looked at Peter. "Like what you see?"

Peter smiled and picked up his penis. He wagged it again. "Need the bra off too," he said again in the same goofy voice.

THE WINTER FOURSOME

"Ugh, it's coming Peter! I was trying to be sexy and take my time." Kristal rolled her eyes and hastily took off her bra in one motion.

Her boobs spilled out and were met with an applause and cat call from Terry. "Woo hoo, go girl!"

"Very nice," Peter agreed. "Terry would ya look at these tits on my girlfriend. What a masterpiece. But, Kris, babe. I'm completely naked and you're uhh… well, you're not."

"Everything?" Kristal asked incredulously.

Peter nodded. "It's only fair," he said as he pointed to his cock.

Terry smiled at Kristal. "He does have a point. But look, the desired effect is happening." Terry pointed towards Peter's stiffening dick. She guessed it to be at least eight inches in length and widening by the second.

Kristal slipped down her sweatpants and little red panties, revealing her thinly shaved crotch. She kept her legs tightly pressed together as not to reveal herself too quickly. She took a seat on the couch and crossed her legs. Her foot with black polished toes bounced in the air.

THE WINTER FOURSOME

"There we go!" she said presenting herself with her hands. "All naked."

"Well, now I'm overdressed," joked Terry as she admired Kristal's perfect body. "Once Donald gets here, maybe we'll join in on the fun."

"God you're beautiful," said Peter as he openly stroked his cock, staring at Kristal. "You both are of course, but Terry's spoken for."

Terry blushed at the unexpected compliment. She watched Peter's hand openly as he slowly moved it up and down his cock, which was almost entirely erect. She took special notice of the defined network of veins running down the shaft. Her pussy was already soaked.

"You're gonna get yourself in trouble over there again," Kristal warned as she smiled at Peter.

He took the hint and stopped stroking. She was right, he probably could have cum again right there on the spot. He sat still, hands on both thighs, dick pointing directly up as he openly stared at Kristal's ample breasts.

"Peter, how many times have you seen her naked? And you still can't keep your eyes off her!"

THE WINTER FOURSOME

Peter shrugged. "Do you blame me?"

"Of course not. Kristal's beautiful. And you two are so sweet together."

Peter stood up and headed for the kitchen to fix the women something to eat. Terry watched him walk away before turning back to Kristal. "He is so big," she mouthed. Kristal just smiled and nodded proudly.

"Can one of you guys give me a hand, please?" called out Peter.

Terry was the first to get up. "You sit. I'll help," she said as she headed for the kitchen. She found Peter with a bowl of popcorn and some cheese and crackers. He had cracked open a bottle of wine and was pouring three glasses.

"Why don't you grab these wine glasses, and I'll get the rest," he said with his back to Terry. She admired his tight, pale butt. Peter was incredibly muscular, she noticed.

As she approached him, Peter spun around unexpectedly and almost crashed into her. She stopped as his throbbing cock jutted against her midsection. Peter immediately held the wine glasses out far so that they wouldn't spill, but in doing so poked his penis deeper into Terry's stomach.

Terry shrieked a bit as Peter jumped back, realizing what he had just done. "Sorry about that! You snuck up on me!" Peter said as he stood in front of Terry.

"Here you go," he carefully handed her the glasses. She took them in her hand and watched his hovering cock the entire time.

"Ahh, thank you," she said before she noticed a wet spot on her t-shirt. "You, uh, you got some on me."

"Got some what?" he asked. Peter's cock had left a large spot of precum on her shirt from when they collided. "Oh, sorry about that, Terry."

"Well, I guess that thing prevented us from spilling the wine, huh?" she joked.

Peter laughed and shook his head. "You're right."

When they returned, Terry noticed Peter stole her seat next to Kristal. She didn't mind, and she sat across from them where she could enjoy watching two beautiful people, both completely naked.

Peter's erection seemed to gain strength as they ate and drank. Terry knew she was openly staring at it, and she knew Peter was catching on to her gaze again. He, of course, didn't mind, and neither did Kristal.

After the trio finished off a glass of wine, Kristal took hold of Peter's cock. She didn't openly stroke it, but just grabbed it as they cuddled on the couch. Terry didn't make mention of it. It just sort of happened. In fact, Kristal was nonchalant about it and carried on her conversation.

Peter was getting his share in too. He repeatedly grabbed a handful of Kristal's tits and slowly caressed her nipples as they drank. He told an entire story to the group as he mindlessly rubbed her nipple with his hand at one point.

Terry found herself becoming more aroused. She was surprised that she was so comfortable with this.

Then, without notice, Peter and Kristal started making out. It was not that they had planned it or even knew it was going to happen. But, before anyone knew it, passion took over.

THE WINTER FOURSOME

Terry watched from her seat with her legs crossed, wine glass in hand. It was a little uncomfortable at first, but the situation quickly felt normal. She was tipsy, but very coherent.

Peter leaned forward on top of Kristal as she sunk into the couch. She spread her legs to make room for Peter's large frame. He licked his hand and then rubbed his cock to lube it up. Kristal, however, used her hand to completely cover her vagina, sending a message to Peter. She wasn't quite ready for that.

Peter took the hint and inched further up her body, placing it directly between her warm and enveloping breasts. Kristal smiled as she squeezed her orbs around Peter's shaft. He was so comfortable as his large balls rested on Kristal's lower chest while his head pressed against her neck.

Terry couldn't believe how big his pulsing penis looked against Kristal's tight little body. She turned and smiled at Terry, knowing full well that she was enjoying the show. Kristal looked back down at her chest and pushed her boobs together tighter. Peter groaned as he rocked back and forth, sliding his his member up and down her frame.

THE WINTER FOURSOME

The slippery, wet sound of his cock against her smooth skin was loud.

From Terry's perspective, she could see Peter sliding his cock back and forth as well as Kristal's tight little pussy behind Peter's butt. Her lips were pink and puffy, moisture leaking out unabashed. A small part of Terry wanted to leap up out of her seat and plunge her tongue into her friend's eager vagina. But she contained herself.

Peter continued thrusting for what seemed like forever. He was mostly quiet throughout the event, save for a few moans and groans here and there. Kristal shifted her gaze from her boobs and his cock, to his eyes, and to Terry. Terry kept quiet as not to ruin the moment, but she displayed a closed-mouth smile the entire time. She wanted to make sure Kristal knew she was happy to be there.

Finally, Peter shifted from his forward position to sit up straight on his knees, cock in hand. "Ok," he said with a strained voice," I'm gonna cum."

Kristal looked up at him with her big, green, beautiful eyes. She pressed her tits together and waited for her man to unload. Peter stroked his cock up and down two full times before pausing at the base.

THE WINTER FOURSOME

The first shot was small. It dribbled out of his cock head and dropped innocently down to Kristal's belly button. Suddenly, Peter grunted very loudly, as he had done so each night before, and shot a massive, double-streamed cum jet directly onto Kristal's face. She closed her eyes and mouth and turned her head to the side. Cum had covered her face.

"Peter!" she screamed out.

But he was just getting started. Terry watched in amazement as Peter stroked his cock, angling it downward to unload three more full cum blasts onto Kristal's tits. He was silent with his mouth dropped open as he tore through his second orgasm of the day.

Terry watched his dick closely as he sprayed Kristal. Five, six, seven blasts, his cock throbbing with each one. She counted the cumshots in her head.

Kristal held her hand up to try to shield herself from the ungodly amount of cum headed her way. Peter grunted again, this time softer as he launched two more small-sized blasts before ceasing. He held his cock tightly at the base as he hunched over with his eyes closed. Kristal lowered her hand and leaned forward to inspect the mess. Just as she did so, Peter moaned as a final thick blast exited his dick and nailed Kristal right in the face.

"Asshole!" she shouted as she slapped Peter on the thigh. Terry and Peter burst out laughing at the unexpected final cumshot to the face.

"I'm sorry babe. You knew the last one was coming though!"

"That was hilarious," Terry said as she stared at the massive amount of semen covering her naked friend.

"Well, Terry, what was it like being a spectator for a boobjob?" Kristal asked as she slowly smeared Peter's cum all around her belly. Peter used the towel left from earlier to clean up. His softening cock hung far below him, brushing against Kristal's legs as he moved about.

"I gotta say," said Terry as she watched Peter clean up Kristal. "I think that was even more than before."

Peter smiled and nodded as he looked at Terry. "I gotta say you're probably right."

Just then, the door whipped open. All three turned toward the entrance. Donald stood before them, covered in snow, wearing goggles and a helmet. At first he didn't see anything. As he quietly took his helmet and boots off, Terry turned to the other two with a look of surprise.

CHAPTER X:
SHOWER INITIATIVE

"Hey babe!" she called out. Donald responded but was muffled as he was still wearing a face warmer. He slowly walked towards the living room and immediately stopped dead in his tracks.

Terry was sitting in the arm chair, legs crossed, fully clothed, holding a wine glass. Peter was hunched over Kristal, cleaning her with a towel. They were both naked. There was still cum everywhere. Kristal's face was caked with it. Donald turned back towards Terry and removed his face covering.

"Umm... okay. Anyone want to explain?"

Donald stood patiently and waited for an answer, specifically from Terry. It was hard for him to be upset. Just yesterday he had received a handjob from Terry in front of everyone, and he and Peter shared an oddly personal interaction in the sauna. There was no doubt nudity and sex was going to be a theme of the weekend. He just didn't quite know how to react while it so blatantly occurred when he was the only one not present.

Peter finished cleaning up Kristal quickly and hastily. Some cum remained on her belly and in her hair. She didn't bother putting her clothes back on but instead sat upright on the couch with her legs crossed. Peter balled up the towel, placed it on the ground, and sat next to Terry. His soft cock, still exposed, hung over the edge of the couch.

"These two are wild is what's going on, babe," said Terry as she smiled up at Donald. "They were just having fun. I'm glad you're home. Come, come. Sit."

Donald hesitantly took a seat in the armchair opposite Terry. A half smile appeared on his face. "So, how did . . . how did this happen again?" Donald gestured towards Kristal and Peter.

"We like being naked," said Kristal as she looked directly at Donald. "Both of us do. So, we got naked! And then this animal couldn't keep his hands off me." She winked at Peter.

"Oh right, Kristal. You had nothing to do with this at all," Peter said sarcastically. Donald glanced down at Kristal's tits as she looked away. They were beautiful, large, and sexy, especially with cum dripping down them and onto her belly.

THE WINTER FOURSOME

He met eyes with Terry, who caught him looking. She felt a small tinge of jealousy enter her mind. And yet, just a minute ago she'd been staring directly at Peter's plump cock. Donald felt his own penis stir, even under his ski clothes.

"So, you guys gonna join us?" Kristal asked. Donald raised his eyebrows, unaware of this apparent plan to be naked again.

Peter took a sip of his wine. He sat leaning forward, legs spread apart. He picked a piece of lint off the shaft as the conversation continued.

"What do you think, Donald? I waited for you to come home. You wanna join them?" The group had already seen Donald naked, but Terry had yet to reveal anything that hadn't been covered by a bikini.

"I just got home, guys. I'm tired. I need to shower. Let me have a drink at least, huh?"

"You know, guys," Peter said. "There's a huge shower room downstairs. Kristal and I could clearly use a rinse off too." He gestured at their bodies.

THE WINTER FOURSOME

He had a point. It was a great shower with plenty of room. It would allow them all to clean off together and for Terry and Donald to get naked without an obvious spotlight. Donald decided he was in favor. He looked over at Terry. "Not a bad idea. What do you think?"

Terry thought about it for a moment. She was so horny from watching Peter and Kristal that she let her strong emotions do the thinking.

"I could go for that."

*****

Terry and Donald undressed outside the shower area. This was where Donald originally first saw Peter's penis and knew what kind of a 'different' weekend he was in for.

"How was skiing?" she asked, delaying taking off her clothes.

"Did you have sex with them?" Donald asked, taking advantage of his time alone with Terry.

She shook her head. "Donald. No. C'mon."

THE WINTER FOURSOME

"Then what happened? Kristal was covered in cum, like a piping bag exploded in her face."

"They had sex. Well, actually they just fooled around. I don't even know how it started. We had a couple drinks and they just kinda started messing around. I guess I should have left the room."

"No, no, no" said Donald as he took off his shirt and folded it on the bench. "It's okay, babe. They're clearly into this stuff a lot more than we are. I know how hard it can be." He got quiet for a few minutes.

"So, did you like it?" he asked, painfully curious.

"If I'm being honest? Yes. Yes, I did."

"Yeah," said Donald, agreeing. "I kinda do too. It's a little exhilarating, huh?"

Terry nodded as she gained confidence. It was nice to get this out there with her husband. She peeled off her t-shirt, revealing her large breasts in a light pink bra. She slipped out of her sweatpants, leaving just her underwear. "You sure you're okay with this?"

THE WINTER FOURSOME

"Babe," said Donald as he pulled his pants and underwear down. His penis flopped out, no bigger than two inches and nestled in his modest bush. He wiggled his penis with his index finger and thumb. "I've done this already. There's nothing left to hide for me." He said with a smile.

"You're right. Okay, here goes," said Terry as she unclasped her bra, letting her large breasts hang delightfully. Next, she slowly dropped her panties, revealing her dark brown bush. She pressed her legs together, careful to not reveal too much for whomever may come down the stairs next.

"Terry, look!" said Donald as he pointed down. Terry's eyes followed his point to see her pink panties on the floor. On the crotch area was a huge wet spot. She quickly kicked it away with her foot. Donald looked back up at her. "You were turned on, huh?"

Terry blushed as she nodded. "It was hot. Like when we listened to them the other night," she said softly.

Although surprised, Donald loved hearing her admit it. His penis responded as his head protruded a bit from its cocoon. "That's pretty cool," he said as he fondled his dick while looking at her smiling. He leaned over to kiss her just as Peter came down the stairs.

THE WINTER FOURSOME

"Okay we got towels and beers! Oh shit! Sorry guys, my bad!"

"Oh, don't worry about it dude. We ready to do this?" Donald asked as he took two towels and beers from Peter.

"Shower time!" screamed Kristal as she appeared behind Peter with her hands in the air. She was still completely naked with cum starting to harden on her stomach. She was clearly a little tipsy already as she danced around in the changing area.

"Donald's naked again!" she sang in a made up melody as she hugged him unexpectedly. Terry's immediate look of disapproval was apparent to Donald as his penis smushed up against her crotch. He could smell the distinctive scent of semen. He abruptly ended the hug and snaked his way out.

"Oh. My. GOD! Look at you!" Kristal shouted as she noticed Terry was completely naked. She stopped and admired her sexy frame, perfect breasts, and long, lean legs. Kristal crossed one arm and rested her chin in her other hand, as if she was studying a painting in a gallery. "Can I just? Can I bottle you up and take you home? You are so friggin' hot, girl!"

THE WINTER FOURSOME

Terry blushed. She wasn't sure what to make of Kristal's enthusiasm, which resulted in both men also looking her up and down. "You're so funny, Kris," she said as she scurried off to the shower. Everyone followed.

The shower had two columns in the middle, each of which had four nozzles. Naturally, everyone gathered around one of the columns so they each had their own stream. The girls chatted as they soaped up while the guys had their own conversation.

"How were the conditions?" Peter asked as he rubbed soap all over his chest.

"Not bad, but I wish I was out there with you this morning. Things were really starting to ice up."

"Yeah, that's why I go so early. Plus, it gets so crowded later too," Peter said as he moved to wash his crotch area. "On the west peak there's this one trail…" Peter started to tell Donald about a specific area he skied through. In doing so, he carefully washed his cock and balls.

Donald was focused on watched him, not really listening to what he was saying. Peter's dick flopped around like a fish out of water as he maneuvered around the area.

THE WINTER FOURSOME

Donald had now seen Peter's dick a few times, but he was infatuated over how much bigger he was than him. The way his massive size dwarfed Donald was incredibly embarrassing, yet a little exciting. He didn't know what to think about the feelings he's noticed this weekend. He looked over at Kristal to freely check out her amazing body. As they chatted, he noticed they were both watching Peter wash his cock and balls. It seemed his dick was a natural attraction.

"...now they don't even allow you to ski over there, but if you take the first path..." Peter continued.

Donald moved onto his own crotch. He was rapidly developing an erection, and the added stimulation by his hands didn't prevent it. He glanced at Terry, who was directly staring at Peter as she washed her vagina. She used her big loofah in long and exaggerated strokes across her pussy. He wondered if she was getting off a bit.

Donald was hard. There was no use. He couldn't control it any longer. He moved on to shampoo his hair. He hoped that if he stopped touching himself, it would go down. But Kristal noticed immediately.

THE WINTER FOURSOME

"Soldier at attention!" she said as she looked down at his sprouting erection. Donald covered it easily with one hand. Kristal giggled.

No more was mentioned of his erection. Everyone ignored it out of respect, but it would not subside as Donald continued to admire the beautiful women as well as Peter's oversized penis. Peter was able to confidently control his erection as he chatted. It was like this was an everyday thing for him. Donald noticed he even casually played with his dick as he hung out with everyone in the shower. Nothing sexual, just fidgeting.

Terry couldn't stop looking at Peter's cock. Seeing the strong contrast between his flaccid dick and her husband's hard cock was staggering. She had given up using her loofah a while ago as it was making her far too horny.

"You guys wanna hang in the sauna after this?" Peter asked as he finished rinsing and turned off his faucet. Everyone agreed and finished showering.

Terry exited, leaving just Donald and Kristal. He watched her eyes glance down at his penis, then back up. She smiled, but didn't say anything. Donald wondered what a woman who gets a ten-inch penis regularly thought of his small cock. They finished their showers in a somewhat awkward silence.

*****

In the sauna, Peter and Donald sat naked facing Kristal and Terry. Kristal stretched out her legs so they rested on the bench next to Peter. She flexed her cute, painted toes as Peter rubbed one of her feet. She remained completely naked while Terry covered up from her chest down. She sat straight up, legs closed, hands by her side. She seemed nervous. She looked at Donald's erection and smiled at him. She then looked immediately at Peter's hefty resting penis.

"So Kristal, when did you first realize Peter has, well, you know?" she asked as she took a sip of her beer.

"Oh. I can answer that," she said as she smiled at Peter. "Funny story, actually.

"So, I'm in Austin at a bachelorette party. And all the girls get, like, one scavenger hunt thing they need to do. And, of course, mine is to grab a random guy's crotch," she explained.

"I like where this is going," said Terry, smiling at Donald.

THE WINTER FOURSOME

"We're standing there in between bars at a crosswalk, waiting to cross. And I see this tall, handsome, muscular guy coming up to me. You were on a bachelor party too babe, right? Wasn't it Jason's?"

"Justin, actually," said Peter.

"Justin, right. Anyway, I walk up to him and start talking. All of a sudden, I reach down and grab him, and my hand is where you'd think his dick would be, right? Like where Donald's would be, I guess," she said as she glanced at Donald's dick.

"But, nope! I get all shaft. And I mean ALL shaft. So naturally, I am in pure shock. My girlfriends and his buddies are dying laughing. But me, I was standing there not exactly sure what I just grabbed.

"So, what does my drunk ass do? I keep grabbing and reach further down to see where this damn thing ends. And what do you know? I find this thing in all its glory," she said as she pointed to Peter's cock.

"Wait, so you guys were total strangers?" asked Terry. Peter nodded, "later that night we weren't though."

THE WINTER FOURSOME

Kristal smiled as she tucked her hair back behind her ear. "We hung out all night. And then, yup, we hooked up. I just had to see it for myself."

Kristal moved her foot into Peter's lap and started playing with his penis with her little toes. "Now he's mine," she said softly as she held it up with her foot.

"I swear to you, every time I see it, I can't believe it," Terry said as she watched Kristal play. Donald gave up on embarrassment. His wife was clearly infatuated with the man, and there was nothing he could do. He looked at his own little cock as it stood up straighter than an arrow. Precum oozed from the tip.

"Watch this," said Kristal as she rested her feet on Peter's thighs. "Peter get hard."

"Really?" Terry asked, eyes wide open.

Kristal nodded. "Just watch."

Peter sat with his arms crossed as everyone, including Donald, stared. He had seen this trick before. Peter's penis expanded rapidly. Within seconds, it stood straight up at ten long and thick inches.

THE WINTER FOURSOME

"Holy shit," said Terry as her mouth dropped open. "That's impressive, not gonna lie. It's like a fucking magic trick."

Kristal proudly laid her feet against his dick on each side like a hot dog bun. Peter was bigger than her feet.

"Jesus, dude," Donald finally said, breaking his silence. "Do condoms even fit you?"

"We have to search for the biggest size we can find, and they do," answered Kristal. "We honestly stopped even trying to use them."

Terry remembered she had seen the box in their bag but kept it to herself.

"Holy fuck," said Donald as he shifted uncomfortably in his seat.

Kristal looked at his dick. "What about you, Donald? How big are you?"

Donald remembered how Peter called him out on lying the other day. Everyone knew it was small, so there was no sense in lying anymore. "Four and some change," he said with a shaky confidence. Peter didn't say anything, and Donald was relieved.

"No way, really?" Kristal asked in a high pitched questioning voice.

"Yes, Kristal. Really," sighed Donald.

"Oh no, no, no Donald, I'm not making fun!" she giggled. "I was just thinking that makes Peter more than twice the size. That's all! Every shape is a fun shape. I just like them all."

Donald wasn't buying her explanation as he sunk back into humiliation. Terry defended him. "I like Donald's dick. It's cute. It gets the job done, let me tell you guys," she said as she winked at him.

"Your balls are huge!" said Kristal as she checked out Donald. "Seriously, look at those things. They're like golf balls." Everyone looked at Donald's balls, hanging loosely in his scrotum on the bench below. He didn't have to move his penis out of the way.

"Do you ever cum a lot?" she asked.

Donald nodded. "I have my moments of explosive power." He said with a more genuine chuckle. He was starting to relax a little more.

"Can you guys stand up real quick?" Kristal asked as she removed her feet from Peter and sat up on the bench. She pressed her chest out, displaying her boobs for everyone to see. She was really taking charge.

Peter and Donald stood up as she asked. "Now face each other," said Kristal.

Peter turned to her, confused, before he obediently faced Donald. Donald did the same. Kristal then rose to her feet and approached the two men. She grabbed hold of Peter's cock with her left hand.

Kristal then grabbed Donald's cock with her right hand. "Look at you." She then pulled the men closer together. "I just want to see something," she said as she positioned their penises next to each other.

Peter and Kristal had been to sex parties. They had a lot of experience in this area. But Donald was completely new to it. Before this weekend, he had never so much as been naked next to a man in a locker room. The first moment their flesh touched, he felt a strange sensation

THE WINTER FOURSOME

take over his body. The situation was so incredibly bizarre and unique, he was inexplicably enjoying it.

Donald looked down and watched as Kristal pressed their cocks together, examining the true size difference between them. Her slender, sexy fingers manipulated their shafts as she compared from every angle she could. Length, girth, and hardness.

"You're like two of him, babe," she said to Peter as if Donald wasn't there. Donald looked over at Terry who sat with her legs and arms crossed, still wearing a towel. She was did not appear to be entranced by this whole charade.

Donald's cock was gushing precum as his arousal intensified. The viscous liquid was smearing all over Peter's cock as Kristal moved them about. Peter didn't seem to care as he watched their dicks glisten in the light. "Sword fight!" yelled Kristal as she pretended to jab their dicks together.

"Okay, okay, that's enough," said Peter as he pulled away laughing. "You've had your fun."

THE WINTER FOURSOME

"You're all wet from him," said Kristal as she slid her hand up and down Peter's cock using Donald's precum as lube. "Terry, you gotta take care of your man!"

Kristal sat down next to Peter and held his cock in her hand while Donald sat across from them, next to Terry. She sensed he was embarrassed but deeply aroused. She knew her husband well enough. She smiled warmly as she finally removed her towel, revealing her luscious, soft breasts. Donald immediately reached out and grabbed one. Terry tucked her dark hair behind her ear and leaned over, taking Donald into her mouth fully.

"Whoa," said Kristal as she watched, holding Peter's hard cock but not stroking it.

Donald moaned as he stretched out his legs as far as they would go in the cramped sauna. Terry deep throated him while fondling his balls with her other hand. Her warm wet mouth going up and down his cock, her head bobbed as Donald closed his eyes and ran his fingers through her hair.

He was so deeply aroused, he felt he was going to cum any minute. He desperately wanted to last, so he tapped on Terry's head indicating her to stop. She kept sucking though. Finally she took the hint and raised her head up, catching her breath.

"No good?" she asked Donald, concerned.

But it was the opposite. It was too good. Donald thought he stopped in time, but the moment had arrived. His body jolted with pleasure as he released a thick and plentiful cum blast out of his penis, through the air, and onto Peter's thigh across from him. Peter bounced out of the way in shock as Kristal burst out laughing.

"Dude! What the fuck?! Friendly fire." he yelled as he stared at the cum on his leg. Terry, stunned, covered her mouth with her hand as Donald jerked himself off. Three more blasts landed on the floor between the couples, and a fourth one landed by Donald's feet.

"Fuuuck," Donald shouted, in relief, as he jerked out a tiny extra bead of cum. "I'm sorry, man."

"Here," said Terry as she removed her entire towel and handed it to Peter. It's okay said Kristal as she leaned over and licked the cum off of Peter. Terry looked in shock as her friend smiled and said, "tastes kinda sweet."

"Unreal, man," said Peter, shaking his head, but smiling.

THE WINTER FOURSOME

"Oh please, Peter," said Kristal. "Coming from the guy who blasts his cum frickin' everywhere all the time."

She had a point, as Peter was known to ejaculate much longer and in much higher quantities than the group had just witnessed from Donald.

Peter watched Kristal finish cleaning him off and looked up at Donald. "How'd that feel, man?"

"Amazing," Donald said, still out of breath. He used his own towel to clean the rest of the mess before holding Terry's hand tightly. She crossed her leg and put her head on Donald's shoulder. Still thinking about her friend licking her husbands cum.

"That was a good load! A fast load too, Donald!" Kristal said, never one to soften her delivery.

"It's hot in here. Should we go upstairs?" Terry asked abruptly, to which everyone agreed.

CHAPTER XI:
DINNER AGAIN

Donald opened the door and let the women out first, followed by Peter. As Peter walked behind Terry, his penis accidentally poked her ass. She turned around to see what it was.

She looked down and smiled. "Careful with that thing, Peter."

Peter held his cock up and out of the way. "Sorry about that," he said kindly.

Donald noticed how Terry was clearly getting flirty with Peter, and it didn't seem like there was anything he could do about it.

Upstairs, they sat around the living room as Peter built a fire in the fireplace. Everyone remained naked. Kristal and Donald moved around the kitchen, making homemade pizza for everyone. Donald's cock had retracted to its two-inch state. As he worked on rolling out the dough, Kristal looked down at his penis.

"He's hiding!" she said teasingly.

THE WINTER FOURSOME

"He's just resting up," responded Donald as he gently tugged on his flaccid dick.

"Resting indeed. He kind of went crazy down there for a second, huh?" Kristal smiled as she concentrated on getting the toppings together for the pizza.

Donald watched her sexy boobs as they swayed back and forth as she moved around the kitchen. When she turned around, he checked out her ass and tugged again on his penis, hoping to get it hard again. Donald thought to himself, *if Terry can flirt, then so can I.*

Peter and Terry sat on opposite ends of the couch, angled towards one another. The fire crackled in the background. Donald and Kristal could see them, but the house was too large to allow them to overhear the conversation, especially over the music Kristal played.

Terry looked over at her husband to see he was preoccupied with making dinner before turning back to Peter.

"I love how your dick just kind of begs to be talked about, huh?" she said as she noticed his long and thick penis standing straight up. "It looks so hard it hurts," she added.

THE WINTER FOURSOME

Peter angled his dick outward and stroked it. "It's really hard right now."

"Could you go again?" Terry asked, curiously. She lowered her voice. "You came twice today. And not even just a little."

"I'm fully reloaded, believe me," he said as he squeezed his dick from the base as if it was a baseball bat.

"That's amazing," said Terry, practically whispering. She openly stared at his cock as if it was a show on a television. "You said it's ten inches, right?" Peter nodded. "What about the thickness? Have you ever measured that?"

Peter shrugged and looked down. "I actually don't think I have. That part never really comes up once I say ten." He said with a quiet chuckle.

"It looks super thick," she said. "Like a big pipe or something," she giggled quietly.

"You can put your hand on it if you want. I don't mind," said Peter as he removed his hands, opening the invitation for Terry to grab him. Terry looked over her shoulder towards the kitchen. Donald and Kristal were facing away from them, talking. She turned back towards Peter with a thirsty look on her face. She leaned over and outstretched her soft hand.

"Here, try here," said Peter as he pointed towards the middle where it appeared to be the most thick. Terry slowly circled her hand around it. Her red polished small fingers and darker skin provided ample contrast to his large kind of pale penis. Peter's warm cock throbbed in her grasp.

"Holy shit," she said as she stared at the massive cock in her hand. "This is nuts."

"No these are," said Peter as he lifted up his heavy balls.

Terry rolled her eyes. She continued to hold onto his cock as she checked on the other two. Coast was still clear. She pulled her hair back with one hand as she leaned in further and stuck her tongue out. She licked Peter's penis tip softly, tasting his precum. The salty, gooey lubricant sent chills through her body as she tasted it for the first time.

She quickly sat back up and released him. Peter was speechless. "Well now?" he said, smiling.

THE WINTER FOURSOME

Terry held her finger up to her mouth. "Shh," she said sensually before leaning back and taking a sip of wine. She turned towards the kitchen. Donald was leaning against the kitchen island, with his back to Terry and Peter. He was talking to Kristal, who was putting toppings on the pizza.

Terry turned towards Peter and spread her legs slightly, revealing her soaking wet pussy. She spread her lips apart with her two fingers as Peter watched closely. She then inserted her middle finger into her vagina fully. As she retracted it, she showed Peter her creamy fluid had caked her finger. She licked it off and smiled before crossing her legs and winking at Peter.

Peter couldn't believe what had just happened. He clutched his cock tightly, thinking he may cum right there and then. But he maintained his composure, responding to her actions by stroking his cock again. He scooped up his own precum from his cock and held out his index finger. Terry checked the kitchen again before leaning in and sucking it off his finger.

The whole exchange took no more than a minute, but the chemistry and sexual tension between the two was very obvious. Terry had to have this man, even with her husband in the other room.

"You, umm... you spilled," said Kristal as she pointed towards Donald's crotch back in the kitchen. He looked down to see a glob of tomato sauce had landed on his dick.

"Oh, shit," he said and looked around for a paper towel.

"Here," Kristal giggled as she tossed him a dish towel. She watched as he cleaned off his cock and part of his balls. "How's he doing down there?"

"All good," said Donald laughing. His embarrassment of being naked had all but faded after the events of earlier, plus the rest of the weekend. He wiggled his cock playfully. As Donald stood facing away from the living room, Kristal couldn't help but notice at the far end of the room Terry and Peter were sitting closer. From her perspective, she couldn't quite see what they were looking at, but she paid no attention to it. She looked back down at Donald.

"It looked like Terry got that whole thing in her mouth, huh?"

THE WINTER FOURSOME

Donald nodded. "Yeah, she definitely did. But it's not like it's," he held up his soft penis, "that hard to do or anything."

"Still, though. It was impressive. I wish I could do that to Peter."

"Maybe if you were a giraffe!" Donald said with a huge grin.

Kristal cracked up. As she laughed, she keeled over, tightening her stomach muscles. Her boobs gyrated as she held them in place with her hand. "You're funny," she said as she stood straight again, smiling while looking at Donald's soft cock. "Wine?" she asked.

Donald enthusiastically nodded, 'yes.'

As Kristal poured them some wine, she again peeked over at Peter and Terry. This time, Terry was facing Peter with her legs on the couch. Kristal couldn't tell what was going on, but she was pretty sure something x-rated. She got a tingle in her stomach as she watched from a distance. Swinging was nothing new to her and Peter, but Terry was one of her closest friends. To share Peter with her would be very exhilarating, but she was not sure how Terry would feel about it. She decided to keep Donald company, since they were having their fun, and have some fun with him.

"Ya know, we don't normally do this in the winter," said Kristal as she pointed to her naked body. "I'm so fat this time of year. I think I ate like a month's worth of food during Christmas." Kristal handed Donald a glass of wine as she lightly rubbed her tight stomach in a circular motion.

"You're crazy if you think you're fat. You're in amazing shape," said Donald as he stared at her midsection. His eyes wandered over her plentiful boobs before venturing to her v-shaped crotch.

"Aww, thanks. You're sweet," she said. She noticed his dick was lengthening. "Donald!" she pointed down. "Are you getting hard again?"

"Sorry, yeah," he said as he concealed his penis with one hand.

"Don't apologize! Don't be silly. I'm impressed actually. You just came not long ago."

Donald removed his hand, revealing his sturdy erection. His balls tightened up in his scrotum. He flicked it down once and let it spring back up before he moved on to put the pizza in the oven. Kristal watched him as he moved about the kitchen. Donald wasn't in great shape, at least compared to Peter, but she found him oddly attractive. It was endearing the way he sprang an erection clearly from looking at her.

"Let me see this real quick," she said, putting her wine glass down. They were far enough from the other couple, she figured Terry wouldn't see. Kristal approached Donald and held his penis with her two fingers. "Wow, he's hard, huh? Feel like you could go again?"

Donald nodded as he watched her manipulate his penis. "I legit could," he said.

"So soft, yet so hard," Kristal commented as she openly stroked his cock. She couldn't help but notice the extreme difference between Peter's and Donald's penises. Donald's could easily fit in her one hand, while Peter needed two — maybe even three — hands. Kristal also noticed Donald's tightened balls were probably half the size of Peter's enlarged bird eggs.

"Not exactly like Peter's, huh?" asked Donald as he watched her hand move about.

THE WINTER FOURSOME

Kristal giggled, "Not quite, no. But I like it."

Kristal stroked his penis. She jerked up and down in a frantic motion. Donald closed his eyes and clenched his butt cheeks. There was something about this kitchen and Donald getting handjobs this weekend. He opened his eyes to see Kristal opening her mouth and going down. Her warm mouth and soft lips caressed his dick. He could tell she was going slow as to not have him cum too quickly. Her boobs were shaking back and forth as she sucked on his dick. It had been years since another woman had seen his cock, much less suck on it. It was so hot. His cum boiled from the depths of his testicles that he hadn't felt in years.

"Fuck," he said as he reached out and grabbed the back of her head. Kristal sucked a little harder and faster, moving her skillful tongue around his dick. Just then, an explosion of cum coated the inside of Kristal's mouth. She continued to suck even as Donald grew weak in the knees. The creamy finish flowing down her throat.

"I didn't wanna cum that quickly," he said plainly, feeling bad. "I was gonna try and take longer to cum but that didn't happen."

THE WINTER FOURSOME

Kristal pulled away, somewhat embarrassed. "Oh my God, I'm sorry. I got carried away." She grabbed a napkin from the table and wiped some of the cum that was left on his dick. "Sorry about that." She said with a sly smile. The situation was extremely exciting to her.

Donald grabbed her hand and squeezed it. "Don't apologize. Thank you for that."
Kristal smiled. "Pizza's ready!" she shouted as she walked towards the living room. Donald followed behind, still possessing a half hard-on from the thought of what just happened. They both carried a pizza and placed it on the coffee table.

Peter was still erect, but Terry looked flushed and frazzled. Donald studied her face. He knew that face. She was deeply aroused at the moment. He guessed it was probably due to Peter.

"Somebody's back," said Terry as she noticed Donald's semi-erection.

"Yeah, I hope none of that's in the pizza," Peter said as he noticed Donald's wagging dick.

Donald laughed as he quickly swatted it away. "Heh. I think we're good, guys. There's definitely none in the

THE WINTER FOURSOME

pizza. Let's eat, shall we?" Donald said as he looked at Kristal, who was now starting to blush.

"This is really good," said Terry as she sampled the pizza. "You guys make a great team!"

"Yeah, we can come up with some things," Kristal said with a smile.

"Have you guys ever had Donatello's in the Back Bay?" Peter asked.

He began telling a story of when he and Kristal went there after a late night with friends. As he told the story, Donald watched him closely. His penis wasn't erect anymore, but it remained an impressive sight as it stretched off the edge of the couch. His story was captivating, but Donald wasn't so sure it was the story that stole the show but rather his big, thick cock in plain sight. He watched Terry's eyes. She was paying attention to the story, but he counted her glancing at Peter's dick seven times.

He noticed Kristal too. He thought that she would be looking at it too, but she was repeatedly looking back at him with a smile. Donald couldn't believe the attention this guy was getting from his wife with his dick. But at

THE WINTER FOURSOME

that instance, he was getting attention as well. This realization Donald's semi-erection throb even more.

Terry crossed her legs and faced Peter as she ate her dinner and listened intently. Donald's viewpoint offered a great side angle of her gorgeous and shapely breasts. Her nipples were so sharp they looked like they could cut glass.

Donald was so horny, he had to get closer to Terry. Even though he wanted to have Kristal. He decided he was done with dinner and walked over to her on the couch. "Scooch," he said as he gestured for her to make some room. Terry slid over on the couch as Donald sat down so that she was now in between the two men. She smiled and winked at him as she grabbed his penis with her right hand. She squeezed it once before letting it go. Donald was so hard, he felt like he'd cum from her single squeeze.

*****

CHAPTER XII:
PARTY TIME

"Okay, okay, you guys," said Terry as she put her empty plate on the coffee table and got comfortable. "We want to hear about these sex parties."

"Sex parties?" Donald asked.

"Mm hmm. Kristal told me they go to sex parties. Now I must know what happens there," she giggled.

"Jeez. You two are full of surprises," said Donald.

"They're not really parties so much as just getting together with other couples and having some fun," answered Kristal. "We like to try new things." She winked at Peter.

"Do you guys have sex with other people?" Donald asked.

"We do!" Kristal answered enthusiastically. "Honestly, Donald. It'd be impossible not to. Once the girls see what Peter's got going on here, he becomes very popular at those things."

"You mean his dick?"

"Yes. They see it and gravitate towards it."

THE WINTER FOURSOME

"You don't mind?" Donald was intrigued.

"I actually love it! I'm proud of my man," Kristal said, again smiling at Peter. "I mean, c'mon, look at that!"

Kristal shifted the spotlight to Peter's oversized cock as Terry happily checked it out again. Not having to be discreet, she leaned forward on the couch to get a good look.

"You really do have a huge penis," she said to Peter as she sat back. She smiled at Donald and held his hand tightly. She didn't want him to feel embarrassed. Peter humbly remained quiet.

"Terry, are you gonna ski again this trip?" Kristal asked, shifting the conversation.

"I may go tomorrow. I'm being super lazy, you guys?"

"Same here. Ya know, though. You could maybe get some skiing in right now by the looks of it," Kristal said with a mischievous look on her face.

Terry was perplexed. "Now?" she asked. "It's like nine o'clock."

THE WINTER FOURSOME

"You've already got your poles in position," said Kristal, prompting everyone to crack up.

"Oh my god, Kristal. You're hilarious," said Terry as she held Donald's hand tighter. Donald glanced down at his leaking cock. He was careful not to touch it, as it felt like a ticking time bomb. Everyone else realized this as well.

"Well, your man is for sure ready to burst again. And I don't mind you taking Peter for a spin if you're interested."

Peter laughed. "Oh, you don't mind huh, Kris?"

Kristal giggled. "Oh please, you mean you wouldn't want this gorgeous woman touching your dick?"

Peter put his hands up. "I'm not saying anything."

Terry turned to Donald. He knew what was coming. "Would you care?"

How could Donald say anything? He already got a blowjob in the kitchen making fucking pizza. There was little left to hide. Everyone was naked. Plus, he had already cum twice in the open. He was in no position to argue anything.

"Down the mountain you go!" he said enthusiastically as he placed both hands behind his head, leaning back.

Terry kissed him on the cheek as she grabbed his dick with her right hand. She then turned sexily towards Peter. As they locked eyes, they quietly recalled their secret moment from earlier. Terry bit her lower lip as she reached over and picked up Peter's meaty cock. It's warm flesh and vast size was still an unfamiliar feeling for Terry.

As she held it, she could feel him growing, inch by inch, until he reached what appeared to be his largest state. The stark contrast of Donald's small penis and Peter's towering cock in her hands was painfully obvious. Terry knew Donald like the back of her hand. She could tell he was about to cum. So rather than embarrass him, she held back from stroking him. Instead, she placed all her focus on running her tiny hand up and down the enormous shaft to her left.

"How's it feel in your hand?" Kristal asked.

THE WINTER FOURSOME

"It's so big and thick. I didn't know dicks got this big to be honest."

"I know, right? Peter, does she feel good?"

He smiled and nodded. Peter had one arm on the back of the couch and the other on the arm rest. He watched silently as Terry jerked him off in front of his girlfriend and her husband.

"Terry, you look good with two dicks in your hands!" Kristal continued. She was eager to make everyone comfortable.

Donald was very quiet. He watched in envy as Terry stroked another man's dick. Her hand had so much ground to cover, and he noticed she was twisting it as a way to accommodate. He looked down at her right hand, stationary at the base of his dick. Her two fingers almost covered his entire shaft. He was so small compared to Peter. Donald looked over at Peter's cock. Before this weekend, he had never so much as looked at a man naked. But he couldn't help but be completely drawn in by the power of this thing. It was captivating. And the woman he loved was seemingly obsessed. He thought about asking Kristal to come over and help him out but decided against it.

THE WINTER FOURSOME

The room was silent when he felt the first pulse. He tried everything from closing his eyes, to focusing on work, to taking deep breaths. But it was no use. Terry wasn't even doing anything to him when the first glob of ejaculate streamed out his tip and onto her hands. He was motionless, holding his breath, desperately trying to hold it in.

'Not so soon!' he thought to himself. But once the levee broke, it was useless. Another shot of cum came flying out his dick and into the air, about six inches high. This time, he grunted. Everyone, including Peter, turned to look over as they saw Donald's cock spasming a third shot of jizz.

"Honey!" shouted Terry as she quickly started stroking, not wanting to waste any of what was left. Donald stretched out his legs and closed his eyes as his dick shot out two more smaller doses, dribbling down Terry's fingers. "Mmmm," she said, somewhat forced. "Does that feel good, baby?"

Donald didn't say anything as he flinched from sensitivity. His orgasm was over and now he was sitting there with a quickly deflating penis and cum all over himself. As the post-orgasm clarity rushed in, Donald felt an overwhelming sense of embarrassment and shame.

"That was a good one, Donald!" Kristal said. "Almost as good as earlier." She said with a smile.

"Yeah, dude, how you feeling over there?" The group was being so kind to Donald. But it was obvious he was feeling like half the man Peter was. The whole penis thing was really starting to get to him. Unmatched in size and stamina. Unable to hold his orgasm in. All the while, his wife very clearly favored another man's penis over his.

"That was awesome," Donald said, forcing an answer. "Quick, but good."

Kristal smiled softly at Donald. She felt almost guilty for him having to waste it, as she could have easily swallowed again.

As the attention shifted away from Donald, Terry released his soft cock and wiped the cum on his thigh. She then used both hands on Peter's cock and still appeared to be insufficient. Peter noticed some white substance was now on his shaft.

THE WINTER FOURSOME

"Natural lube, huh?" Peter asked as they both watched Terry use Donald's cum to jerk him off.

Kristal loved watching other girls with Peter. She mostly admired the look of pure lust and desire in Terry's eyes. She knew his cock was mesmerizing to both women and men. Watching their reactions fueled her own desires and made her want him even more. But she was also turned on by Donald's ability to get rock hard back-to-back.

As Terry worked on Peter, Donald sat naked with a shriveled penis, feeling vulnerable. He was angry with himself for cumming so soon, jealous of Peter, embarrassed to be soft again, and seriously wishing that Kristal could have been there for him again. But, now he had no choice but to try to enjoy the show in front of him.

"Jesus, my arm is starting to hurt!" Terry said as she looked at Kristal. "This is a workout!"

Kristal laughed as she sat curled up in the armchair. She was blatantly fingering herself with her hand between her legs.

Terry checked on Donald. She noticed he was watching, but frowned. "You ok?"

THE WINTER FOURSOME

He smiled and nodded. "Just enjoying the show."

"I love you," she said as she turned from her husband to focus on another man. Terry increased her pace with both hands as she feverishly masturbated the huge cock. The cum on his dick had all but vanished at this point, but his head was leaking enough precum to continually lubricate.

After some time, it was clear Peter was going strong. He had stayed fairly quiet save for a few soft moans. Still, Terry could sense Donald was uncomfortable. She decided it was best to stop. "Damn! I don't know if I can go any longer with this thing," she laughed. "Kris, you want to tap in?"

Kristal, flush and bothered, rose to her feet and walked over towards Peter. Her hand was very obviously wet as she was covertly masturbating in her chair. She stood before the three of them contemplating where she should sit.

"You. Up," she said as she directed Peter to stand up. Peter obeyed and now stood next to her. His dick was throbbingly large, looking bigger now than it had all weekend. He slowly stroked it while he waited. Even his own large hand was dwarfed by its size.

THE WINTER FOURSOME

Kristal took his seat but instead laid down, her head resting on Terry's lap. Terry looked down into her eyes. "Oh, hello," she said amusingly.

"We're gonna fuck now," Kristal stated plainly. Peter laughed at his girlfriend's impressive command. Kristal grabbed Peter's hand and guided him on top of her. She spread her legs wide. Donald watched closely as she opened her soaking wet pussy for Peter. He felt his own cock showing signs of life again.

Peter first rested his hard dick on Kristal's stomach as if he was showing off. It stretched all the way to her tits, its head sandwiched between her large orbs.

"Holy shit," said Donald, the first to react.

"Whoa," Terry added. "That's huge."

Donald gently cupped Terry's boobs as they both marveled at the impressive imagery before them.

"Is that gonna fit?" Terry asked, genuinely curious.

"Oh, it fits," said Kristal as she smiled and stroked Peter's penis. "Just watch."

THE WINTER FOURSOME

Peter licked his hand and took hold of his big cock, lubricating it with his saliva. He first pressed his large cock head into Kristal's wet and inviting pussy lips. Her moist and pink labia easily spread to accommodate its oversized guest. Peter's large and bulbous head slid in with ease as he pressed harder to fit another few inches. Kristal smiled and closed her eyes as she welcomed his cock inside. She slowly rubbed her clit with one hand while rubbing one of her nipples with the other.

As Peter continued to advance his dick, Donald regained an erection. He moved his left hand from Terry's breast to her vagina which he noticed was incredibly wet at this point. He easily slid three fingers in. With his other hand, he jerked off. Terry started moaning immediately. How Donald wanted to put his dick in Kristal's mouth while she was getting fucked.

"Ohhh God! Yes! Fuck me!" Kristal started to scream as Peter pounded her with at least three fourths of his cock. The screaming was familiar to Terry and Donald by now as they had listened to it night after night. "Mmmmm, fuck Peter. Oh fuck. Yes! Yes! Fuck, you're so huge!"

"Jesus, look at that," said Terry as she stared at Peter's cock nearly completely inside Kristal. "It's so big. That's so fucking hot!"

THE WINTER FOURSOME

Kristal couldn't respond as the arrival of her orgasm took complete control over her. She convulsed over and over again as Peter's cock initiated a powerful response.

Donald watched Kristal's orgasm and his wife's reaction as he stroked his now fully erect penis and fingered his aroused wife. The scenario was strangely familiar, as it was only two nights ago they both masturbated to these two having sex. Now, here they were right in front of them.

Peter continued thrusting, remaining mostly quiet the whole time. He was now completely inside Kristal with each sliding motion. She spread her pussy apart with her fingers as she leaned her head forward to watch. Her mouth was wide open as she moaned with delight.

Peter supported himself with his hands on the cushions as he dripped sweat all over her. His breathing had increased and he let out a few grunts and moans. Donald assumed Peter's moment was approaching and thought this might be the perfect time to test the waters. He stopped fingering Terry, and whispered to know one in particular, "can I put it in her mouth?"

THE WINTER FOURSOME

Terry had yet to help out as she was too preoccupied in watching the other couple. She shouted, "yea... sure!"

Just then Donald got up and leaned in past the sweat dripping man with the huge cock and shoved his penis in Kristal's awating mouth. She moaned and grabbed his hips to pull him in closer. Terry was completely aroused by the display but had not yet processed what was happening.

"Oh my god, you guys," said Terry as she blurted out an aroused comment. "Are you both gonna cum?"

Peter looked up at Terry and made eye contact as he penetrated Kristal. He smiled and nodded. "I'm gonna cum. Watch out guys."

Donald looked to her and gave an affirmative head nod as well.

With that, Peter grunted loudly as he pulled his dick out and launched a huge thick rope of cum across Kristal's body and Terry shrieked. At that moment Donald grunted and filled her mouth with his cream as well. Kristal gave a loud moan.

THE WINTER FOURSOME

Peter kept stroking as another two blasts splashed across Kristal's perfect stomach.

"Fuuuuck!" Peter shouted as he angled his spewing cock down. But it was not effective, and the force of his next blast bounced off Kristal's breast and landed on Terry's thighs. Donald looked closely at the thick consistency and volume of his latest blast. It was impressive.

Donald had been frantically trying to remove his own now sensitive dick the entire time to miss the blasts. As he had reached his third orgasm of the day. He leaned his head back watching his penis still devoured by Kristal's beautiful mouth. As Donald came, Peter continued to shoot loads across Kristal's body at an impressive rate. One landed directly on the corner of Kristal's mouth, and slid down Donald's cock. But Donald was mid-orgasm and didn't want to stop. He kept thrusting in her mouth as another load from Peter landed on his thigh.

Peter's last two shots canvassed Kristal's stomach harmlessly as he sat back out of breath, surveying the scene.

"Holy shit," Terry said. "How'd that feel you guys?"

THE WINTER FOURSOME

"Amazing," the three of them said in unison as they caught their breath and laughed.

Kristal looked up at Terry as her head was still in her lap. "Did you cum too?"

Terry smiled. "I did," she lied. She was close to her climax before her husband jammed his dick into her friend's mouth.

As Peter caught his breath, he peered over at Donald and eyed his softening dick. "How you doing over there buddy? Whoa, looks like you had some fun too?"

Everyone glanced at Donald's face, and he looked drained. He held up the shot of cum from his thigh for everyone to see. The large glob fell from his hand onto his shrunken penis.

"Wow, Donald!" said Terry, in a tone that he knew was angry. "Even after you just came!" Before Donald could say anything, Kristal piped in, "yeah he came a lot in the kitchen. Mmmm, you taste... really good." She said closing her eyes savoring the flavor of his cum in her moth.

THE WINTER FOURSOME

Donald knew Terry was slightly upset about the kitchen comment. He suspected Peter might be too because no one had discussed it before hand. But Peter let it go. Terry was impressed, turned on, and clearly enjoying herself. But she was starting to get angry. Her post-orgasm clarity was starting to come through. He couldn't believe that he has another man's cum on him and wasn't that freaked out. A more impressive cock and clearly more impressive load.

By this point, Terry was completely overtaken by anger.

"So, wait, wait, wait... you gave my husband a blowjob in the kitchen. When did this happen?"

"Umm... right when we were making the pizza," Kristal said with a tone of apprehension. "I didn't think you would mind since it looked like you and Peter were getting comfortable." Kristal lied. She knew her friend would probably not like it.

Terry let out a nervous laugh, "so, YOU gave MY husband a fucking blowjob over pizza and didn't think to ask me first?" Terry's voice had become louder, and the tension in the room was becoming palpable.

THE WINTER FOURSOME

"I mean you didn't think that you should ask first?" said Terry

Then Peter joined the conversation, "well Terry, you didn't ask before you licked my tip and sucked precum off of my finger."

The room grew deathly silent.

"I'm gonna turn in guys because this is fucked up" Terry said as she stood up. Everyone watched as her large boobs swayed from the frantic movement.

"Whoops," said Kristal as she covered her mouth, trying not to laugh. "I guess I pissed her off, huh?"

"You go, babe and I'll clean up," Donald said, sensing Terry was eager to get out of there. Everyone was silent as she ascended the stairs and slammed the door of their bedroom.

Kristal turned to Donald, concerned. "Is she okay?"

"She'll be fine. Probably just overwhelmed by what happened tonight. Ohh, wait a minute, she licked it?" Donald said as he looked at Peter.

THE WINTER FOURSOME

"Hey dude, no disrespect, but she was way into it. I didn't say anything about licking. That was all her. I just said she could touch it."

"Well, I mean fuck, I can't say too much about it, I guess. Especially after the kitchen."

Kristal laughed, "yeah, I think you're toast. Hell, we both are. I hope she knows we were just having some fun."

Kristal shrugged. "It's only ten thirty. Let's hit the Jacuzzi again!"

Donald looked at the empty stairs, "yeah, I guess I might as well. I won't get any sleep once I go in there." He said with a chuckle.

Meanwhile, upstairs, Terry was wide awake and heard them head to the hot tub. Her anger was starting to boil. She was not a violent person by any means, but at this moment she saw red. She thought to herself, *I licked just the tip of his dick, and played with myself while he watched. I mean I only jerked him off after asking if it was okay. He got a full-on fucking blowjob in the kitchen making my dinner. Those fucking assholes. I can't believe that bitch would do that. I have to do something, say something, at least confront them. You know what...*

THE WINTER FOURSOME

I'm going down there!

Made in United States
Orlando, FL
30 July 2024